FANTASY AND

ROY FULLER was born in Failsworth, Lanca
poetry at a young age, his first poem being published in 1928. He qualified
as a solicitor in 1933 and worked for many years at the Woolwich Equitable
Building Society, ending his career as the head of the legal department. From
1941 to 1946 he served in the Royal Navy, becoming a lieutenant in 1944.

Though he wrote several well-received novels, Fuller was most famous
as a poet, publishing his first collection in 1939 and many others over a more
than fifty-year career. He also wrote several volumes of memoirs as well
as books for children. He held the prestigious Professor of Poetry chair at
Oxford and was awarded a C.B.E. and the Queen's Medal for Poetry in 1970
and the Cholmondeley Award from the Society of Authors in 1980. He was
married to Kathleen Smith, and their son, John Fuller, is also a well-known
poet and novelist. Roy Fuller died in 1991.

ROY FULLER

Fantasy and Fugue

VALANCOURT BOOKS

Fantasy and Fugue by Roy Fuller
First published in Great Britain by Derek Verschoyle in 1954
First U. S. edition published by Macmillan in 1956
First Valancourt Books edition 2024

The Valancourt Books name and logo are federally registered trademarks of Valancourt Books, LLC.

Published by Valancourt Books, Richmond, Virginia
http://www.valancourtbooks.com

ISBN 978-1-960241-22-1 (trade paperback)
Also available as an electronic book.

Cover by Roderick Brydon
Set in Dante MT

To A. E. Shrimpton

Lucky the lawyers with some leisure time:
Golf for the innocent; for the guilty, crime.

One

I

When I awoke I imagined that I was in my old room in my father's house, and looked in vain for the familiar crack of light at the top of the door opposite the foot of the bed. One of the terrors of my childhood seized me: I thought that during the night I had gone blind. Then I saw, through the gloom, the white door to the right of the bed, and recognized the bedroom of my flat. The clock on the bedside table said 9.20, and faintly illuminated by its little glowing dial was the cylinder of sleeping pills. I had the slight hangover they always induce. It must be morning.

I lay back on the pillows and closed my eyes again, steeped in the depression of unformulated – of unformulatable – worries which lay concealed in the day ahead. The sheet rubbed my face uncomfortably: I felt my chin and found a surprising growth of whisker. I could not have shaved yesterday – or even the day before. What had I been doing?

I got out of bed, drew the curtains and opened the window. Light and the noise of the traffic drenched the room. I looked in the wardrobe mirror as though at the portrait of a stranger whose deeply interesting reputation had preceded it. The light-blue eyes were set in skin the colour of a cream rose: the rest of the face had a glassy pallor, the dark hair tousled, the jaw already becoming formidably bearded. I took off my pyjama jacket and found my body oddly unchanged. The invalid's face owned an athlete's biceps, marked pectorals, flat belly. This was indeed Harry Sinton who regarded me, however damaged, however deranged. I stood there in the indecisive mood which I recognized had become habitual.

What was I thinking about? There was a dream – of a great room, men I did not know, a precipice – lodged vaguely and no longer frighteningly at the back of my mind. There was a vista of days behind me, blank, similar days. I tried to remember my friends, the office, the squash club, my brother Laurence. They were all as remote as a period of existence severed by a long war. In the absence of other stimulus there was nothing for it but to go through the conventional motions of living. I went to the basin, turned on the hot-water tap, and tightened my razor.

2

Washed, shaved, and dressed, a simulacrum of normality, I stepped into the corridor as apprehensively as into a room of expectant strangers. But only the little angular men on the Persian runner greeted me. The white paint on the walls still looked new: opposite me was the Wyndham Lewis drawing of two cats I had bought at Oxford: Mrs Giddy had placed the vacuum cleaner ready for use when I should wake: someone had even bought daffodils. All that was lacking was my own participation in this life – a life that had once been mine but which I had somehow left behind: the elaborate but unfinished chapters a novelist finds in a forgotten drawer.

As I walked towards the kitchen I actually felt the muscles tighten round my solar plexus: merely the prospect of speaking to my housekeeper alarmed that other man inside. I took the deliberate breath that always seemed to ease the tension: that I remembered to take it meant that the tension was still amenable to control. This was a comparatively good morning, perhaps. I knocked on the kitchen door and put my head round it.

'Good morning, Giddy.'

She was at the sink. 'Good morning, Mr Harry.'

'No breakfast,' I said. And then quickly to drown her horrible, maternal moan of protest: 'I'll have some coffee. Lots of it.' I shut the door on whatever boring thing she was going to say, and went into the sitting-room.

Here again the calm, moderately luxurious existence confronted me incongruously — the spacious civilization turned up by the spade of the crisis-torn archaeologist. I could not conceive now the state of mind that had enabled me to have the fireplace wall painted that exact shade of mulberry, to choose the canary upholstery, to instruct the joiner to make the spaces of the bookshelves elegantly and extravagantly tall. Even after Christmas I must still have been in touch with this world of the gross senses. Or had Laurence arranged all this for me? No, there was a bookshelf left carefully barren of books which held a silver-mounted golf ball, a framed photograph of the Middlesex C.C. 2nd XI, a little medal in a plush-lined case, that could have been done by no one but me. Perhaps it was these trophies of the so-called healthy life, not the Kafka, the Hölderlin, above and below them, that had led to my present state. Once it had pleased me to read Proust while I waited my turn to bat, to stand at the bar contributing my rude story with Hopkins under my arm. Now this dichotomy in my taste seemed evidence of weakness, not strength, both poles sinisterly extreme.

Had I really been before those terrible Christmas events merely *l'homme moyen sensuel*? Yes, as I looked back, I saw that I had quite happily lived in my father's house; gone every day to the office, to the small and highbrow publishing firm that Laurence had founded and I had joined; played my games; attended my parties, films, concerts; talked; enjoyed food, drink, sleep. Just as before that I had quite happily been the lieutenant, the observer in naval aircraft; the President of OUPS; the prefect, the boy who went in first wicket down; the vigorous second son. And now, by a freak of fate, all was guilt and anxiety. Only the phenomenal strength of my former character enabled me to pierce, in moments like this, the fog of bewilderment, irrationality, amnesia, that coiled round me, and to see how far I had gone down the slope of neurosis. Neurosis was the polite word. My essential normality was struggling like a cat, more and more feebly, to release itself from the arms of an alien and terrifying giant. It must have been nearly three months since I played any part in the firm's affairs, over two months since I had abandoned the doctor's ridiculous tonics and orthodox advice, weeks – how many weeks? – since I had left my flat. Like a man dying from a long disease, my active world was slowly contracting.

Lost in these alarming thoughts, unmindful of the mortal

danger, I walked slowly to the window. This flat, in which I had lived since I left my father's house in Esher Square, was at the top of an old building at the junction of Luxor Street with New Oxford Street. Below were three floors of offices and a shop which sold dim and scratchy gramophone records of the Golden Age of Song. Luxor Street strikes New Oxford Street obliquely, and my sitting-room was at the apex of the angle, the windows making a narrow half-circle at which I could stand and watch the traffic far below, like packages on a conveyor belt, rolling up from Holborn. At first I used to stand there often, in day-dreams in which I sailed away from the dangerous, populated cities, breathing the magic syllables of my name and the wind taking them back from the light-suffused prow to where, on a coil of rope, the ragged beautiful cabin-boy slumbered. Later I watched more and more infrequently.

Now in the glass of the window I saw that face again, the pale face of a valetudinarian who still cannot believe that he is condemned for ever to his house and bed, his former life gone. Perhaps it was this tragic reflection that made me look quickly through it to the street below, to the people walking, stopping, crossing, free as the single electron. I must take a Veganin: the inside of my head, like a model used by a lecturer on anatomy, was in several only moderately well-joined pieces. As always, my emotions were as near the surface as a recent widow's.

The traffic was halted at the lights. A figure crossed in front of it – the figure of an elderly bourgeois wearing a black homburg, carrying a rolled umbrella. The smoke-grey clouds had blown over sufficiently to let the March sun, in an aperture of the palest blue, send a gleam to the wet streets. The figure reached the near pavement. There was something so familiar about it that I closed my eyes involuntarily as though the light from it had been a dagger.

To escape the pain of what I had seen, I turned and walked rapidly across the room. Not until I had foolishly kicked over a little kidney-shaped table and the china ashtray it bore had been shattered on the boards, did I open my eyes. The table rocked on the floor with the noise of some great decelerating clock. The cigarette burned my fingers. Yes, this was the specific nature of my malady: this was the recurrent terror, the reason for the sleeping tablets, the growth of beard, the scapegoat's existence.

From where I stood, startled and trembling, the deceptively innocent window frame held nothing but the sky's moving washes. In the room there was no one but myself, and no object that was strange or dangerous. Here was my chair, with its back to the light, and the cigarettes and the books, the unaccepted invitations to private views, the table of persistent periodicals.

And then – as a calamity is remembered in the moments of waking – I remembered that from the window to the traffic lights was only a lethal pistol shot, a not too difficult shot for one with time to aim and who owned and could use a .45 service revolver. What a mad fool I was to think that mere not-looking could absolve me! I rushed back to the window and stared along the street. Blessedly, the old man was stolidly there, unshot, walking safely towards me. And now I could see quite clearly that he was a stranger.

With shaking hands I lit another cigarette, watching almost with detachment the old man trailing his umbrella along the pavement, and blew a powder of smoke gratefully against the glass. I looked at him with the growing pleasure of one who has dreaded some horrible sight, but at last has screwed up his courage to face it. Two girls passed him, then a taxi. When he came into view once more he was walking towards the branch of Boots on the far corner. He moved across the pavement, up to the shop, and then went in at the door.

His disappearance set my pulse going again. I told myself that he was in the shop, alive, to repair the ravages of civilization, to buy magnesia or a denture brush. In a few moments he would come out again, still alive. But the pulses still throbbed. I tried to imagine that I had no responsibility for the continued existence of this man. But it was no use: on each of my hands, which now grasped the window ledge as I craned forward, the four sinews to the knuckles gleamed yellowish-white with strain. Like putting a lid on a boiling pan, my brain made its feeble effort of ratiocination. Let us assume that the man never appears again, that the worst has happened, that I have murdered him. The police trace the line of the projectile. It could have come only from this flat, this room designed for murder. The police find that there are two people in the flat: the housekeeper, Mrs Giddy, and the tenant, Harry Sinton. They immediately discard as a suspect the seventy-year-old woman.

So once again I faced the agonizing problem of finding myself an alibi. I looked at my watch: it was ten minutes past ten. I had to have an alibi from ten o'clock. My imagination quickly peopled the room with police. 'What have you been doing all morning, Mr Sinton?' they asked. What had I been doing? Rousing myself from a drugged sleep: trying to remember where I was, what I had done yesterday, the day before: recalling old guilt. Hopeless. The agitation knocked urgently against the lid. And then it came to me clearly what I had to do. I must put the clock on the mantelpiece back to ten o'clock, call in Mrs Giddy, unobviously but incisively draw her attention to the false time. When the police came she would be able to say: 'At ten I brought Mr Sinton his coffee. We chatted for several minutes about my poor sister in Guildford. . . .'

I really thought about this seriously, embroidering it, feeling good about it. And then, as one suddenly sees through a daydream of heroism or riches, I saw through its puerility, and started to toil back up the enormous slope towards the relatively rational state I had been in before my victim appeared. A murderer can get away with his crime only by demonstrating beyond question the utter normality of his life. The exaggerated protestation of innocence, the elaborate alibi – these are equally fatal. Calm ambiguity: that is what has always baffled the police.

I righted the anatomical table and turned on the switch of the radio. As I collected every splinter of the ashtray, the sane progressions of the *Gold and Silver* waltz projected themselves into the room. The sports trophies gradually gained ascendancy over the hysterically-bright spines of the poets, the hearth-brush over the brain-grey ceiling, the heavy cigarette box that had belonged to my father over the Dufy lithographs. Now to establish a normal, easy contact with the world: should I telephone Miss Hind at the firm, or simply wait for Mrs Giddy?

And then I saw the pieces of ashtray in my hands, irremovable as blood, as fatal a clue as the body. I looked round wildly for

a hiding place for them. Everywhere were the unobvious apertures of guilt. I ran to the windows and edged one of them open.
As I cautiously put my hands out to drop the china fragments
into the gutter that ran a few feet below, I saw my quarry – the
elderly, respectable, professional, innocent man – emerge alive
from the shop. In that moment of relief, too incredible to be
pleasurable, I stayed rigid, my fists clenched in the chill air. Then
I brought them in, closed the window, and dropped the pieces
of ashtray on the window ledge. I saw that now there really
was blood on my hands. Something that I thought was laughter
started shaking in my stomach, but when I brought it up I found
to my astonishment that it was a few hard sobs.

That was how I had been for several months. And I was as
incapable of comprehending my state as a rat transferred to a
physiologist's maze. I only knew that I was dangerous.

3

'Your coffee, Mr Harry.'

'Thank you, Giddy. Put it on the small table.'

'And here's the paper come at last. Ten o'clock! It's too bad,
isn't it? I'll call round at the shop when I go out, and complain
again.'

'Do.'

'Oh dear. Now what's happened to that nice little ashtray?'

'I had an accident with it.'

'Oh dear. What a pity! I did so like that little ashtray. Well, acci-
dents will happen even in the best regulated families.'

Mrs Giddy swept up the pieces of china into her overall. At
such times as this I could not believe that she was simply an
ignorant, well-meaning, kindly, unimaginative old woman of the
lower orders. The banal tone of her conversation, her irritating
tricks of speech, seemed designed not only to exacerbate my
condition but also to mask a sinister interest and understanding.

She said: 'Are you all right this morning, Mr Harry?' There it
was: surely the black eyes were glittering with morbid interest,
not solicitude. And 'this morning': did she mean that yesterday

morning had contained some frightful incident of my neurosis?

'Quite all right, Giddy,' I said, and forced myself to add: 'Thank you.' I felt as stiff and awkward as a lay figure with the effort of hiding my cut hands from those inquisitive eyes, so practised in finding out secrets. How quickly she had connected the shattered ashtray with my shattered health! She wallowed in the interlinking of her life with others – it was her recreation. She threw out a dozen tentacles and planted the suckers on the tenderest parts. And so far as I was concerned she knew too much. In the past my situation had forced me to confide in her, as one is forced during military service reluctantly and with shame to reveal one's private life to a superior nincompoop. It was agony for me to remember how close we had sometimes been and not so long ago; that occasion when I had broken down completely I simply refused to go over, but all the same it loomed behind our every encounter as though we had once been lovers. What an utter fool I had been to choose – or let Laurence force on me, perhaps – an old and boringly privileged family retainer for my housekeeper! Even her physical appearance had become hateful – the straight grey hair cut incongruously in a school-girl bob, the sallow complexion, the nose that drooped as though the cartilage had been removed.

'Will the cold pie do for lunch, Mr Harry?' she asked.

'Admirably.'

'You didn't eat much of it last night. And shall I order another dozen Guinness while I'm out?'

'Please, Giddy.'

It was one of the absurd conventions of my present state that a bottle of stout with my lunch and supper was helping to lead me back to recovery. She turned and sidled from the room on her flat feet. In that last instant there had been a momentary change of expression on her face, a look of – what was it? – disgust. No, fear. I got up agitatedly. Had she, after all, observed my hands? Or been spying through the keyhole at my attempt on the old man? Suddenly I could not bear to be left as lonely as her fear would make me. I wanted to call her back and establish a normal happy bond, yes, even with her.

And then, as was typical of my malady, my mood changed. I went inside the walls of myself, blotted the blood off my hands with my handkerchief with the sullen self-pity of a punished child, and threw myself into the easy chair. I sipped the coffee: like the cigarette, it mingled with and extended my emotions. No, my life was not to be endured. And as though I were reading the closing pages of a novel I quite clearly saw the thing ending. Constantly now I experienced the sickening feeling that arrives at the finish of a night of insomnia, when dawn shows through the curtains and the illusion that sleep may yet come is finally dissipated, and the long day has to be faced with nerves and body irremediably weakened.

But there must come a dawn when the sufferer decides that his strength has all gone, when no barrier stands between him and the often-imagined but hitherto unapproached act. I put down my coffee cup, turned off the radio and stood in the midst of my possessions, looking at them almost as though already I had a different order of existence from their ordinary solidity. I tried to imagine just precisely when it would end, this life I had made for myself which, in spite of its material richness, was wearing thin like an empire in decay. Every day drew behind me its own watertight door that increased my insulation from the normal past. Every day had its eccentricities, fears, fantasies, that created for me a consciousness utterly different in kind from that of other humans. My so-called friends had ceased to telephone, unconcernedly letting me drop out of their lives and thoughts like a disgraced second cousin.

The Times lying on the chair arm was like the case-history of an obscure genus of insects: I saw with a kind of interest that the date was March 1st. When I opened it the rumours of war in its chaste headlines affected me no more than the advertisements for commodities I did not want. On one page the world, on another the nation, on a third the family – I had no part or interest in any of these organizations. I turned the sheets over to the one which recorded the activity of the individual, the only activity which had the slightest power to stir my chronic introspection. Last night four men had played Mozart, Brahms, and Fauré. Another was exhibiting the result of three years' solitary confinement with pigments. The queer verse of *Hamlet* had once again been spoken in a theatre.

Beside these reports from the world of the anti-social and
unhealthy ran the cold obituary column. A Spanish prince, his
diplomacy long ago exploded, made a last dignified, absurd
appearance. The expert in naval gunnery of 1914-18 had died
after twenty years on retired pay. The third entry briefly recorded
the career of Max Callis.

> Max Samuel Callis, the poet and novelist, died suddenly in London
> yesterday. He was 33 years old. Born in 1916, he was the younger
> son of Ebbutt Callis, the Liberal publicist. While he was still at
> Oxford, he wrote a biography of his father (who had died in 1934)
> which called attention to itself as much by its unfilial sentiments
> as by its wit and period-sense, both of which were considerable.
> In the late nineteen-thirties Callis lived in various Mediterranean
> countries and published two books of verse which gained for him
> a high place among the ranks of the younger poets of the time.
> He went to the United States shortly before the outbreak of war,
> and his novel, *Campus Pie,* had the background of his experiences
> as lecturer in English at an American women's university. He
> returned to this country in 1944. But it will be as a poet surely that
> Callis will continue to be remembered. His last book of verse,
> *The Microbe in Command*, was felt on all sides to be disappoint-
> ing, but his earlier poems about Greece and Cyprus cannot be
> left out when stock is taken of the decade in which they were
> written. Their mixture of clear lyrical imagery and what can only
> be called surrealist thought was quite original and one of the
> definite though lesser influences of the period.

I went on staring at the print after I had read it, horror branch-
ing through me. The images of my encounters with Max Callis
flapped past obscenely, like an amusement arcade peep-show.
'Died suddenly in London yesterday.' So that I should never read
again of that death I crumpled the newspaper into a tight ball
and pressed it into the heart of the fire. As it slowly blackened I
disintegrated it with the poker. I saw nothing else but Max Callis
– the squat body, the large head, the close hair like dark pumice
stone.

To try to batten down the thought that I knew would force
itself out at last I attempted to recall when I had last met him.

It seemed a very long time ago: before my incarceration here, before Christmas even. And then with a momentary reassurance I remembered. It was the party that my firm had given when we published Callis's *The Microbe in Command*. It must certainly have been before Christmas, before my brother had moved into 7 Esher Square, because I clearly recalled encountering Callis in the pink-painted sitting-room of Laurence's flat – Callis swaying a little with too many gins, adjusting his bow tie with podgy hands, making an impertinent remark in his high voice. Yes, that was my last meeting with Callis. I could not have seen him since.

I rose from the fire and walked about in a quite convincing imitation of a normal man who had just received the news of the unexpected death of an acquaintance. Poor Callis, I said to myself. I had never taken to him but that was no reason for gloating over the fact that he had been cut off in his prime. *The Microbe in Command* was a rotten book, I thought, but Laurence was probably right when he had insisted on doing it: Callis might very well, had he lived, have recovered his earlier talent. Yes, 'poor Callis' was precisely the right reaction.

4

Ten minutes later the curtain fell again and I saw the futility of trying to reason out my innocence. Of course I had met Callis at the party, but how could I know that that was the last time? Since Christmas, reason had not governed my actions. I forgot facts, remembered illusions, and though I had tried to render myself harmless in this fortress of a flat I was my own master. I could, like Hyde, have come and gone on errands that my Jekyll-self knew nothing about.

Callis was dead, and the conviction grew and grew, until it filled my whole existence, that I had killed him. I must have seen him since that party, seen him yesterday, seen the hateful body lying dead, the bow tie disarranged, the fat hands extended, the huge head lolling. And yet I could not fix this clear vision into the pattern of yesterday. Indeed, yesterday had no distinctive pattern at all – it and the other days stretched back as indistinguishable as railings.

The room was very quiet, so quiet that it began to frighten me. Outside in the hall, on the stairs, at the entrance in the street, surely the authorities were silently waiting for me to give myself away. It brought me out in a sweat to think that all unconsciously I had lain the night through in my bed, spent the morning in foolish trivialities, while the whole time – like the incubation of war in a period of thoughtless peace – disaster had been ready to fall.

Was it already too late to do anything? I wondered if Mrs Giddy knew about those who were waiting to trap me. Certainly there was that ambiguous look she had given me, and her offer to order the Guinness was an offer which promised a normal future for me too obviously, a bluffing offer. She could not be trusted to be ignorant. I must try to get away from her: that was the first and obvious move.

And then since I could not remember, I had to discover how Callis had been killed: create an alibi for a set of events I knew nothing about. I had to find a memory for myself and then erase that memory by a false memory. What a fool I had been to burn *The Times*! On another page there might have been facts about Callis's death, and facts were my only salvation: I had to learn not to be afraid of them. In spite of a deep-seated sensation of sickness, as though I were poised at the start of a race, I began to feel at the prospect of action, a species of confidence. After all these weeks of apprehension the blow had fallen at last, and terrible as it was it had not annihilated me: there was a bridgehead of fortune left from which I might yet break out. In this new mood I realized that the police must still be ignorant of the murderer's identity, otherwise they would have been here long ago. I had killed cunningly – or perhaps gratuitously, on the spur of the moment. In the latter event all I had to do was to discover the attendant circumstances and sit tight. Systematically I rummaged my memory for all I knew about Callis. It was very little, I found, when I had brought it to the surface, but with growing excitement and apprehension I saw that it provided me with a start.

I opened the door of my sitting-room a little and listened. A low dreary noise, of Mrs Giddy singing *Bless this House,* came from the distant kitchen. I went quietly into the hall, got my hat and coat from the closet and put them on. The image in the long mirror, attired for the street, seemed a stranger. I went to the hall door, turned the knob of the yale lock and pulled gently. To my alarm the door would not budge. I put my strength into it, then saw that the bolt of the mortice lock was home, and remembered. The key, naturally, was not there. I stood with embarrassment pricking my eyes, like a child who has got himself ready to go out and then been denied.

I took off my hat and coat, put them quietly into the closet and tiptoed back to the sitting-room. I stayed by the door for a long, agonizing minute and then walked with loud steps into the kitchen. The singing stopped: Mrs Giddy, on her knees by the cooker, turned her head towards me.

'Ah,' I said. 'Not gone out yet?'

'No, Mr Harry. I'd thought I'd just do the kitchen first. Did you want something?'

Perhaps too calmly I said: 'Giddy, where's the key of the mortice lock?'

She rose agitatedly. 'Dear me, did I forget to lock it? I'm terribly sorry, Mr Harry, terribly sorry.'

'No. The door is locked.'

She looked puzzled. 'Now it's all right, Mr Harry. I've got the key quite safe.'

'Where is it?'

'Why, it's right here in my overall pocket.' Her voice had lost its concern: now it was humouring me.

'I'd like it, please.' I held out my hand abruptly: this was the way I'd planned to get it.

Her voice changed again and she gave a wipe of embarrassment to her boneless nose. 'What for, Mr Harry?'

'I want to go out, of course.'

She did not know whether to smile or look stern. 'Now, Mr Harry, you know I can't give it to you.'

'Of course you can give it to me.' My irritation shook my hand so much that I had to lower it. She had found her expression – the sad, faithful expression of an ill-treated dog.

'But you told me not to give it to you,' she said. 'Never to give it to you.'

'Oh nonsense, Giddy.' I started to bluster. 'Do you think I can stay in this place for ever?'

Old Faithful dug her paws in further: one had to admire her conscientious stubbornness.

'But, Mr Harry, that was exactly why you had the mortice lock fitted, so I could have the key and you couldn't go out.' She was right, of course: I had been out of control and desperately afraid in the streets I should do someone a violence.

She continued: 'Now why don't you go back and listen to the wireless and I'll bring you some more coffee. You know it used to do you bad to go out. Why upset yourself again?'

'Giddy, I'm quite better, and I want that key.'

'I'm sorry, Mr Harry. I can't give it you, I really can't.'

'Don't you understand, Giddy? All that absurdity is finished with. I'm perfectly well and I want to go out. I'm changing the whole arrangement, as from now. I shall keep the key of the mortice lock myself in future.'

'But, Mr Harry, it was only a fortnight ago you had the mortice lock done. You told me then never, never to give you the key, however much you pleaded for it.' Just below the roots of her hair a few beads of perspiration had started. Her hand was deep in her pocket, holding on to the thing.

I fought down my growing alarm. I had never taken this obstacle into my calculations. 'Giddy, please try to understand,' I said as quietly as I could manage. 'It's absolutely essential that I go out. I've some business to do of the utmost importance.'

She had a good answer to that. 'If it's business, Mr Harry, why don't you ring up Mr Laurence and let him attend to it?'

'It has nothing to do with my brother,' I said furiously. The moment I raised my voice she took a step backward, putting the corner of the cooker between us, and I could tell that she was not listening to a word I said. My God, I thought, she is frightened again.

If I did not take the most meticulous care I was going to be trapped, locked in here through my own frailty until the police discovered my guilt at their leisure and came to collect me for the hangman. How clearly I saw the chain reaction characteristic of murder, potentially endless when once triggered! For now, if it became necessary, I would kill Giddy without a qualm. Bash in her stupid yellow face, crack her stupid gold-rimmed spectacles. But first of all, since it was less dangerous, I would try acting a little part. I sank down on the kitchen chair and pressed my hand across my brow.

'I'm sorry I was angry, Giddy,' I said. 'Of course, you're quite right. As always, Giddy. These are just the circumstances in which you have to hang on tight to the blessed key. I'm afraid I'm rather over-wrought.'

She came round the gas-stove. It was like casting for trout. I summoned up all my wit and patience. 'You see,' I went on, 'I've just read in *The Times* that one of my greatest friends is seriously ill. . . .'

Her face relaxed into sympathy: she adored illnesses. I spoke gently, sanely, convincingly, telling her that her duty could be relaxed on my good days, and that, obviously, this was one of them. I reminded her of how much I had improved under her excellent care. After all, nervous breakdowns didn't – mustn't – last for ever. Part of the cure must be, in fact, fresh air and an occasional change of surroundings. I saw her hand emerge from the overall pocket: it did not hold the key yet but it would.

Behind her, the row of cacti on the window sill, my contribution to the decoration of the kitchen, raised their assorted and crude symbols. On the table before me, next to her coffee cup, was her open library book. She was a great but imperfect reader, and sometimes talked to me of her favourite authors, prominent among whom was the popular novelist she always referred to, mistaking the gender, as Vera Stacpoole. I remembered thinking at Christmas of her that the crises of one's life are always peopled with such comic characters.

'And so,' I said, 'I really must inquire personally about my friend's health. . . .' Marinated by the abject confession I self-loathingly made, Mrs Giddy gradually became pliable and tender.

Fifteen minutes later I pushed the key into the lock. Even then it occurred to me to wonder how I had managed to steal and replace the key when I got out yesterday, but the sight of the stairs which led down to the street made me so timorous that I could not pursue the thought. Those stairs, and then the bustle and landmarks of the street, seemed as remotely familiar and significant as a long-last revisited haunt of childhood.

Two

I

Where Shaftesbury Avenue runs up into New Oxford Street there is a curious little oasis, formed by the irregular conjugation of buildings, where cats sit and street sweepers have a quiet drag. The oasis bears trees and call boxes. I made for a call box: it would never have done to use my own telephone.

Was there still, at this stage, an element of *play* in my actions? Though I was very distressed, was there a thought at the back of my brain that this was a nightmare which my sane, conscious mind could with just a little more effort wake me out of? I do not know. The steps that turned me from a fugitive from my own obsession into a fugitive from real events and pursuers were so gradual that I cannot mark any dividing line of increased urgency and alarm.

Certainly in the telephone box I was a disarray of nerves. I could scarcely get my hands to select the right volume of the London directory, let alone turn the pages and find the vital name. And I had to keep glancing up through the glass at the passers by, who were equally a menace to me as I was to them.

I was looking for Clarence Rimmer's number, for the only fact I could remember about Max Callis useful to me now was that Rimmer had once told me that they both lived in flats in the same block. Rimmer was a novelist and critic and my knowledge of him was limited to encounters at parties. It was a tenuous connexion but the best I could make.

Rimmer was in the book, I found at last. The address was 14 Sickert House, with a Flaxman number. It looked as though he hadn't moved: I prayed that Callis hadn't either. I dialled the number and a woman's voice answered.

'Is Mr Rimmer there?' My voice cracked in the middle of the phrase.

'I'm afraid he isn't.'

'Could you tell me where he is?'

'Who is that speaking?' The voice was guarded and behind it I could hear a child crying.

'This is Harry Sinton.' I could think of no reason for lying and an unknown name would immediately drive the voice back to the child. I added quickly: 'Is that Mrs Rimmer?'

'Yes.'

'I think we have met, Mrs Rimmer. I'm Laurence Sinton's brother.' I did really remember her, a rather large, fresh-faced girl.

'Yes, of course,' she said.

'Do you know where I could find your husband?'

'Well, as a matter of fact I think he's gone to a book sale at Sotheby's. I'm afraid I don't know where he's lunching.'

'Sotheby's. I could probably catch him there.'

'Yes, you probably still could. Is it urgent? Will you leave a message in case you miss him?' The wifely nose smelt money for her old man.

'No, it's not all that urgent,' I said. What message could I leave? 'I'll phone again if we don't meet. Thank you all the same.'

We made our good-byes, and I came out of the box. My watch said twelve o'clock. I had no idea how long an auction at Sotheby's was likely to last, but lunch time was dangerously near and I could see Rimmer slipping out of my grasp. I had a nerve-racking walk almost to St Giles Circus before I found a free taxi.

2

Just through the screamingly unobtrusive entrance I saw a girl carrying a file of papers, obviously an employee, and asked her where the book sale was. She said it was up the stairs and through. The traffic jams and adverse lights of Oxford Street

had given me a vile ten minutes, but her calm assumption that
the auction was still on injected a powerful shot of confidence.
I went up the short flight of stairs and through a gallery of glass
cases and dim paintings. This led into an auction room, well lit
by a skylight. In front of the auctioneer's rostrum was a large
green baize-covered table surrounded by a double row of chairs.
The auctioneer was a gentlemanly individual in a grey suit with
matching hair and whiskers. He was saying gently: 'Number two
hundred and forty-eight. I have a bid of three pounds.'

There was brief silence and then a man lounging at the table
said: 'Three ten.' As the bidding continued I searched the faces
round the table. They were all of them, I thought, the faces one
sees at the back of secondhand bookshops—elderly faces with
obsolescent-type glasses, middle-aged faces with unfashionable
moustaches, youngish faces with hooked noses. Dealers to a
man. In some of the seats against the right-hand wall and standing near me round the door were some obvious amateurs – a
fawn waistcoat or two, a monocle, a Kensingtonian *mode* – but no
Clarence Rimmer. I was starting to panic again.

'Seven pounds ten shillings. Boxall and King,' said the auctioneer, and passed on to the next lot. There was a rustle as everyone
turned over a page of the catalogue. And then, in the corner of
the room to the left of the entrance, a man leaned forward to
examine the books in the lot which one of the attendants was
carrying round for inspection, and I saw behind him Rimmer's
unmistakable figure. Unhurriedly and with exultation I started
to edge my way towards him. He had managed to hoist his great
bulk on a long cupboard which on this wall projected from under
the book shelves, and that was why at first I had missed him.

'Number two hundred and fifty. Can I have a bid, please?'

Rimmer had a flat, fat, red countenance and a heavyish brown
moustache. His straight hair came half over his forehead in a Hit-
lerian lock. I suppose he was about forty. He was a rather good
novelist and a better critic. I scanned his face surreptitiously,
trying to divine whether or not he would help me. He had a reputation for being recklessly honest, and very rough in his cups.

'Number two hundred and fifty-one.'

Rimmer raised his head from his catalogue with a studied air of disinterest. The bidding went in leisurely stages from five to eight pounds and then stopped. At this moment Rimmer said 'Eight ten' and looked back at his catalogue. His words seemed to set the bidding off again and it finished at fourteen pounds without his having uttered another word. As the lot was knocked down he looked up, caught my eye and gave me first a nod of recognition and then a grimace of self-conscious disappointment. I grimaced back with amiability.

The sale was ending. Most of the extraneous figures had now drifted away, leaving the hard core of professionals round the table. Nothing prevented me from moving sociably closer to Rimmer. The auctioneer called out a wrong lot number: he was jestingly corrected in a perky cockney voice by one of the seated men. There was a general laugh. The serious business of the day was over.

I took the opportunity of saying to Rimmer: 'I wondered if you remembered me.'

'Of course,' he said. 'How are you?'

'Quite well. It seems a long time since we met.'

'Yes,' said Rimmer.

The last lot was bid for: there was a general stretching of legs and a hum of talk.

'Are you free for lunch?' I asked Rimmer. I hoped I was concealing my anxiety. He slid off the cupboard to his feet with a thud.

'Yes,' he said reflectively. 'Yes, I am.'

'Perhaps you'd lunch with me.'

'Thank you very much. That would be fine.'

'Excellent.' I made as though to move towards the door.

Rimmer said: 'I'm afraid I've got to pay for a lot I did manage to buy. I shan't be very long.'

'Of course,' I said, as though I had all the time in the world.

'It was Symonds's *Renaissance in Italy*. I didn't really want it but the bidding stopped at a pound and I couldn't resist saying twenty-five bob. After all, three and six a volume, you can't go wrong.'

'No.'

Rimmer moved slowly towards the cashier's cubby-hole by

the side of the rostrum and got in the queue of payers. I followed him.

'Now the Nonesuch Dryden I did want,' he continued. 'You heard me poke in eight pounds ten. But on the whole the prices have been absolutely fantastic, haven't they? Fourteen pounds for the Dryden! And by no means in exceptional condition.'

'Fantastic,' I said. It was astonishing to me to find myself involved in this trivial life of books and money after my long sojourn in the life of my own mind.

Rimmer paid over his twenty-five shillings and said he would collect his purchase on his way home. Going down the stairs I said I thought we would go to my club, which was the Sheridan, and where we might just be in time for the joint. He said again that that would be fine. In the taxi I thought he would be sure to mention Callis, but he only asked me how my brother was.

I said: 'Very well, I think. I haven't seen him for a little while. I've been ill you know.'

Rimmer turned his pale-blue eyes on me. 'I didn't know. Sorry to hear it. You're looking thinner.'

'Yes, I've lost weight.'

'Wish I could,' he said.

The taxi squeezed along Jermyn Street. Surely it was sinister that Rimmer hadn't opened up about Callis's death. The man was lying dead in the same building. Could I have given myself away to Rimmer by approaching him so directly? At any rate I wouldn't betray myself further: I resolved not to speak about Callis until Rimmer mentioned him. While I thought all this Rimmer had rather sunk into a stupor, his bulk flung back on the worn leather, his thighs completely filling his trousers. Perhaps like me he felt the strangeness of our sudden companionship.

I made my effort. 'I enjoyed your essay in the *Review*,' I said.

Rimmer looked as though he had been wakened in the middle of the night.

'You know,' I added, 'your investigation of the first use of words like "breasts" and "thighs" in English fiction after the Victorian reticence.'

'Oh yes,' said Rimmer. 'That. It appeared rather a long time ago, didn't it? I'm afraid I wasn't with you.'

'Sorry. I haven't been keeping up to date with things lately.'

Rimmer, too, made an effort. 'Glad you liked it. It was an attractive subject for research. But it really needed one of those American university johnnies with a card index and a big endowment – I only skimmed the surface.'

Mercifully the taxi then drew up outside the Sheridan.

3

With a draught of claret I forced down another mouthful of pâté and tried to cover with my knife and fork what was left on the plate. More would choke me. Rimmer was ploughing through his portion in his painstaking way, his face a shade redder, his brow becoming greasy. The great pictures in their dirty gilt frames towered oppressively over us: above the dark panelling the high walls were hung with crimson paper. We had one of the small tables; in the centre of the room at the communal table was the usual crowd of publishers, actors, writers, editors and businessmen, all looking the same. I had placed myself with my back to them because some knew me.

Our conversation had not managed to find any further flights. 'One could,' Rimmer was saying between mouthfuls, 'investigate the post-14–18 novel on similar lines. Find out precisely when and how it developed a social conscience. And not only that – one could, I suppose, discover all the preliminary hints of the change in attitude. The first touch of anti-semitism, the first serious mention of Marx, the first non-comic proletarian character, and so on.'

'Fascinating. You ought to do it.'

Our waiter came up to the table: it was the young pallid lisping one called John. 'I've managed to save two roast beefs for you, sir,' he said to me.

Rimmer looked at him and said: 'Good.'

'For a long time,' I said, 'I've wanted the firm to publish a series of novels of the twenties and thirties – the half-forgotten ones, I mean. Early Isherwood, for example. And brilliant things like *Afternoon Men* and *About Levy* that if it hadn't been for the

war – the second war – would still have been in print.' What I
wanted to remind Rimmer of was the fact that I was a director
of Laurence Sinton, that we published books, that we published
Max Callis.

It was too subtle for him. 'The only pâté in London not made
of horse,' he said.

The waiter returned and announced with ridiculous pride: 'I
got some roast potatoes for you, sir.'

I said to Rimmer in a burst of exasperation and confidence:
'Food gets worse. Really I can eat hardly anything these days. And
I have fearful indigestion.' I regretted the remark immediately,
for Rimmer looked at me sharply, as though I had betrayed some
psychological maladjustment. I must be careful not to show any
abnormality. 'I blame it on my housekeeper though, rather than
the Minister of Food,' I went on, trying to rescue myself. 'She's
not a cook at all. A superannuated housemaid I inherited from
my family when I set up an establishment of my own.'

Immediately I had uttered these words the club dining-room
vanished and I was sitting again in the dining-room of my father's
house among the gigantic furniture, its dark polish reflecting a
ghastly something from the snow-loaded trees outside the windows. From the heavy metal of the wall lights depended the shining spheres that came out every Christmas. Upstairs the nurse
was bending over the dead. I had come into the room for a few
moments' escape, but Giddy must have seen me. 'Let me get you
a drop of brandy, Mr Harry,' she said in the hushed tones that
everyone in the house had automatically been using.

I swam painfully upwards through these stifling memories and
clutched the decanter of claret. 'More claret?' I said to Rimmer.
He had started on his beef: time was passing horribly quickly. I
must take risks if I was to save myself. As I raised my glass I said:
'Don't you live in the same block as Max Callis?'

He did not rise and denounce me but simply wiped his early-
film-comedy moustache. 'You saw that he was dead?' he asked.

'Yes, I read something in the newspaper this morning.' It was a
triumph to phrase this so non-committally and utter it in a quite
flat tone.

'It must have been suicide,' said Rimmer, assuming tantalizingly that I knew all about it. 'Curious thing – he wasn't the type at all. I don't mean that suicide is confined to a type but that I shouldn't have thought that Callis cared seriously enough about anything to take such a serious step.'

I was conscious that my knife and fork were poised rigidly above my plate. I made an effort to use them. Rimmer went on: 'I can't say I liked him – but I probably liked him more than most. I didn't know him well, though for about a year he lived only a couple of flats away from me. Were you a friend of his?'

'No. But we published him.'

'Of course you did. Well, he's a loss to you, I suppose, though I think he'd written himself out as a poet. I bet you didn't sell many copies of the *Microbe* thing. All bits and pieces, and very thin bits at that. Maybe that's why he killed himself.'

'How did he . . . ?'

'Kill himself? I don't know.' Rimmer put his knife and fork together and emptied his glass. 'Somebody told my wife – '

The waiter's martyred girlish voice broke in: 'There's cabinet pudding, sir, and Neapolitan cream, and some stewed fruit.'

'I'd rather have cheese,' said Rimmer.

'Yes,' I said. How could Rimmer not know the manner of Callis's death? Was he toying with me after all?

The waiter said: 'Would you like some nice Danish blue, sir?'

'Yes,' I said again. I felt the subject floating away on these trivial tides. 'Extraordinary,' I said to Rimmer, hoping to stay it and not knowing how. 'Extraordinary.'

'Had your firm anything of his on the stocks?' Rimmer asked.

'I don't know.' Rimmer would think me mad. 'As a matter of fact since my illness I've had a complete holiday from work.'

'Good idea. No sense in overdoing things.'

'Of course, I'm quite fit now. I shall have to get back to the grind.'

'Yes,' said Rimmer. 'Yes.' His tone was certainly humouring.

The waiter returned. 'There was no Danish blue left, sir.' He paused for his effect. 'But I managed to get you some Camembert.'

'Oh, that will do,' I said, wondering why his face fell and why he brightened at Rimmer's smile. Did he, too . . . ? With what

seemed to me enormous presence of mind and regard for the
conventionalities I ordered coffee and two glasses of Madeira.
That I could bring to mind such things was strong evidence of
my sanity and control. The waiter bent over the table conspirato-
rially. 'Shall I see, sir,' he whispered, 'if I can find some fruit cake
for you?'

'Cake?' I repeated in bewilderment.

Rimmer said: 'That would be splendid.' The waiter smiled
wanly and went off.

Rimmer laughed. 'I don't know how you can be so cruel to
that poor waiter, Sinton.'

'Cruel? Am I being cruel?' I smiled with relief. Rimmer was
genuine and nice: I could trust Rimmer. 'I really haven't been
able to make head or tail of him. All this cake business.'

'He's trying so hard,' said Rimmer, 'and he's such a defeated
figure. One of those very old shambling waiters in the making.
God knows what tyrannies he's had to bear back in the kitchens
to get that beef and the Camembert – and now the fruit cake.
There is a peace on, you know.'

'I'll be kinder to him,' I said. Suddenly I was full of confidence:
the cunning murderer; reckless, but cunning. I smeared a lot of
Camembert on a piece of cream cracker. 'You know,' I launched
out, 'I've often thought that a novel might be made out of the last
day of a suicide. A day of crisis, of the intensest feeling, during
which every motive of the suicide's life is played over again – for
the last time and with the most luscious orchestration. Even
themes from childhood as well as those of the events precipi-
tating the debacle. The novel would simply follow the suicide's
actions and thoughts and show the absolute inevitability of
self-destruction. The inevitability following not only from the
hideous pressure of the proximate facts but also from the long
formation of the suicide's character. It's just the sort of thing you
might do, Rimmer.'

He fell for it. 'Very interesting,' he said politely. 'Yes, it sounds
my cup of tea. But I could get no material from Callis's life, if that
was what was in your mind. I can't think of a single thing about
him that might have predisposed him to suicide. Except lack
of money – but the Callises of this world don't kill themselves

because of that. And as for what you call proximate facts – I never
even saw him during his last days.'

'You didn't?' I couldn't prevent the note of dismay. I felt my
confidence vanish as quickly as it had come: all this elaborate
encounter – the telephone call, the acting, the unending food –
was a complete fiasco. Where did I go from here?

'No,' said Rimmer. He handed me a cigarette and inserted
another beneath his moustache. 'His way of life was a bit irregular, as you might have guessed. He made a habit of sleeping on
other people's floors for one thing. The body of Max Callis was
just as much an aftermath of parties as full ashtrays and half-
empty glasses. I guess he was on a bender before he did it and
that's why we haven't seen him at Sickert House. Can I light your
cigarette?'

I dazedly put the cigarette between my lips.

'Poor Callis,' Rimmer went on. 'When one knows that he is
safely dead one can think back with a tolerant, pitying mind on
those drunken stupors and those frightful black fingernails.'

I pulled myself together: Rimmer must know something.
'Well, I wonder whose floor it could have been that last time.'

'Fay Lavington's, perhaps.'

The blood left my face. To hide the ghastly mask I knew I must
be presenting to Rimmer I dropped my cigarette on the floor and
bent quickly to fumble for it. I saw the dragging yet mincing feet
of the waiter approach the table, and heard the lady-like voice
flute complacently: 'I got the cake, sir.'

4

As I pulled myself upright Rimmer was saying: 'Though it was
more likely her bed. You know Fay, of course. Everyone seems
to know Fay.'

Yes, I knew her: it was true, everyone knew her. But I remembered the time when for me she was merely a face at parties – a
face to which one's eyes kept returning as to one's own reflection
in a near mirror. Her features were distinguished only by their
extreme regularity, her hair and eyes only by their brownness.

Away from her one could not recall what she looked like: with her one could never gaze long enough at the angle her nose made with her brow, the length from chin to throat that at first seemed excessive, the forehead that curved outward so boldly from her straight hair. I even remembered when I imagined she had a mind to match her face.

At later parties I was able to place her more exactly. First she always used to come with an editor, and then with a painter. She held her glass in both hands, the little fingers outstretched, and to drink inclined her head rather than the glass. I began to be able to identify some of the clothes she wore and a thick silver chain she sometimes had round her neck. Once I had been one of a group around her. Somebody was talking about a bad performance of *Boris Godunov.* Fay said: 'Oh, Rimsky's adorable given any old how.' I flinched as though I'd seen a wen on her cheek and even on her behalf blushed a little. Some unpleasant man – perhaps it had been Max Callis – said: 'Rimsky didn't write *Boris.*' Fay giggled and said, ambiguously: 'Wretch!' without turning a hair. What a bloody fool! I had thought, turning away.

And then, after I had joined the Navy, there had been a party at Laurence's flat, at which I had been very tight. Towards the end of it I had found myself with Fay, her hangers-on miraculously absent. 'You don't know who I am.' I kept saying in my drunken stupidity. She said at last: 'Oh yes I do. You're Laurie Sinton's little brother.' 'No I'm not,' I said. 'I'm Captain of the Heads.' I laughed a great deal at this witty jest and then relapsed into morose self-pity. 'Laurie's got out of it all right, hasn't he?' I said. 'Laurie's far too ancient for the Forces, my dear,' Fay said. 'He's only five years older than I am.' Fay regarded him where he stood on the other side of the room pouring gin. 'Well,' she said, 'he's getting very matronly.'

We were sitting together on a sofa. 'Isn't it a rotten world?' I said. 'Filthy,' she said. I saw suddenly that she was really giving me her attention and my eyes filled with ginny tears. I reached for her hand and found my hard grip returned. 'Let's get out of here and have some rotten filthy food,' I said. 'Come on then, sailor,' she said.

I remembered – or imagined I remembered – stopping on the

way to the restaurant, the London buildings powdered violet in
the moonlight, the drone of a single aircraft above, and kissing
her, but nothing more of the evening, nothing of what she said
or what I felt. No doubt I had passed out somewhere and she had
abandoned me. I remembered only waking next morning in my
bedroom at Number 7 with a hangover and a sense of loss. That
day, the last of my leave, I had spent like an adolescent boy, haunt-
ing the places where I might meet her, unable to bring myself to
ask Laurence – or anyone – where she lived.

After the war our relationship had once more been the chance
encounter, with nothing said on either side more than a casual
remark. And then last June, on holiday in Switzerland, I had met
her walking on the Brahms' Quay at Thun. The painter was with
her and a rather dim friend of the painter's who was in the British
Council. She had greeted me with bewildering warmth and at
dinner that evening in their hotel in a little square at the top of
the town I had been persuaded by her to go with them into the
mountains. The two men had been indifferent but had offered no
objection.

Then had followed an extraordinary and agonizing week.

During the days the painter painted, producing his ugly but
quite fashionable canvases of contorted rocks and peasants. The
friend oscillated between the painter and Fay and myself. But
the friend's presence or absence really made no difference to the
absurd state of affairs that came to exist between Fay and I. We
uttered nothing that was committal. Sometimes, looking over the
great grey and green bowls of the valleys we dumbly entwined
fingers, cigarettes smouldering in our free hands. We stretched
out beside the village's tiny lake, ploughing through the party's
pooled library, eating Toblerone. We walked to other villages and
drank beer on wooden balconies, hens clucking below, the children of the house gazing silently at Fay's rather bizarre clothes.
In the *pension* at night, under the thick eiderdown, while the
friend groaned in his sleep in the other bed, I wretchedly strained
my ears for the noises of Fay and the painter in the next room.
During every such night I determined to leave them the next day,
but every day seemed to hold out its little hint of some sort of a
solution. In the end we all went back to London together.

Then I began calling on Fay. It appeared that she was living alone. Certainly the painter had disappeared and she talked about getting a job. But the pattern of our affair – if it could be dignified with such a name – was already set. Sometimes she smiled at me as though I were ten years old: I waited hours for her in bars: I lent her odd pounds: I saw her with a man who was something in films and then with another who was something in advertising. She explained these acquaintances as having to do with the elusive job for which her schemes were so grandiose and her qualifications so meagre. There would come every now and then a day when she would be kind to me and all my jealousy, shame and exasperation would be cancelled – so that it could work up again to the moment when I resolved in vain to stop seeing her.

All this went on into the late autumn. If it had not been for my father's illness it would have been going on now.

5

Rimmer was looking dubiously at the cake. 'Well, it will soak up the Madeira, anyway,' he said, but quietly so as not to hurt the waiter's tender feelings.

'Callis was having an affair with Fay Lavington, then.' I forced out the words.

Rimmer took a cautious bite of cake. 'I don't know about an affair. I saw them in the Corydon a couple of times. It didn't look a wildly exciting relationship – Fay doing her nails and Callis studying a pint tankard with glazed eyes. But then he was always like that with his women. She came to his flat sometimes, too.'

'I wonder if she was with him that last day.'

'I wonder,' said Rimmer. 'You know *you* ought to write this suicide novel: the theme fascinates you, I can see. This cake is better than it looks.'

'I've no creative ability, I'm afraid.'

'That's the first essential in a publisher,' said Rimmer.

Clearly I had to get away as quickly as possible. Rimmer could tell me nothing more: indeed, he had told me nothing that had not already been there in my subconscious. For an astonishing second I *saw* my mental processes with detached clarity. How on earth had I been able to suppress from my consciousness the fact that Fay had been in love with Callis and that that was my motive for killing him? I had known, must have known. There had been nothing fantastic in my panic and flight from my flat. As if to confirm this diagnosis my heart ached with helpless jealousy. Fay and Callis in the Corydon, in the flat: Callis's drunken boorishness, his filthy nails – the images sent a wave of nausea through me.

It all fitted together. First the censor in my mind had erased the knowledge of my jealousy so that I should fail to find a motive for my murder. Then the memory of the murder itself had been cancelled. If I hadn't had the intelligence to understand this I should have been consistently innocent and insane. My lawyers would be able to plead a 'mental blackout', and I would smile gently under cross-examination, my subconscious firmly clutching my guilt, never to give it up.

But I was not mad: merely a murderer with the unbalance of all murderers. I was mad only in action, not motive. My jealousy and violence, swollen to monstrous size, had lain inadequately chained. What I had to do to save myself was uncover the circumstances of the murder as I had uncovered its motives – and then get myself out of them with a cunning equal to my other evil qualities.

The dining-room was emptying: I could escape plausibly. 'I'm afraid I must rush away,' I said, looking at my wrist with unseeing eyes.

Rimmer smiled. His face was glowing, the face of a happy man who has lunched well and who does not anticipate dyspepsia. I looked at him with incredulous envy. He said: 'Thank you very much for an excellent lunch. We must meet again soon.'

'Yes,' I said. 'Yes, we must indeed.' My duplicity even amused me. I called up the waiter with a splendid control over the meaningless customs of the normal world and signed the bill. I added a final effective touch by saying to him: 'Thank you for looking after us so well.'

Was it only my imagination that saw tears spring to the waiter's eyes? I had a momentary pang for the ordinary simple existence that was so near at hand but which I could never again enjoy. I managed to leave Rimmer not too obtrusively while he was at his ablutions.

Three

I

As I hurried down the steps of the Sheridan I was looking for a taxi. Then I realized that I must make my movements impossible to trace: eventually I should be a fugitive if I was not one already. I turned into Lower Regent Street and let myself take the pace of the people who moved along its pavements. When I had come out of my flat at first the closeness of many humans after being so long alone had frightened me. I had looked at every face carefully for the sign of the oppressor or victim. But now that I knew past all self-deceit of the one murder of which I was in truth guilty I could nearly ignore them.

Outside the Lyons I stopped dead and stared at the meat pies and cellophane packets of sandwiches which took on, like the incongruous symbols of a poem, the arbitrary meaning of imagination. What if I had given the whole thing away to Rimmer, if that dark horse had now emerged from the Victorian lavatories of the Sheridan and were already on the telephone to the police? All those questions about Callis's movements, about Callis and Fay, about Callis's death – mustn't it have been plain to Rimmer what they amounted to? I crossed the road, laboriously reconstructing the entire lunch. Not until I was in the Haymarket did I convince myself that most of the damaging questions I had never, through caution or fear, spoken aloud. And, after all, how should Rimmer know of the threads that bound me to Callis, still less of the furious character that hid itself behind the innocent exterior of the young highbrow publisher with a good war record, the member of the Sheridan, the flannel suit of clerical grey?

By the hoardings of the whips and bosoms of the latest films I caught the bus. When Whitehall had been left behind and it had begun to take on its own characteristic route, the feeling of the past crept over me as though I were revisiting my old school or my training establishment. This was the way I had been so often until that sad Christmas Day, and traversed always with an emotion which was part excitement, and part pain. Would Fay be in? Would she be alone? Would she be nice to me? The pubs, the stores, the milkbars and banks, the untidy sky-line of the river's south bank, were all hung round with their particular aura of despair or hope.

Gradually I forgot that I was going to her only to try to rediscover the facts of Callis's death, forgot my need of an alibi, forgot all my anxieties except the old supreme one of loving her unrequitedly. The pain of it returned as a longstanding tooth-ache returns and is almost welcomed because it ends suspense. I thought, as I had often thought before, that it was not true that one cannot love for long if it is not returned. Love is fed not only on satisfaction but also on the crumbs of imagined promises and the mere absence of positive denial is enough to keep it hibernating for years.

The bus stopped by a church: in the narrow graveyard at the side was an almond tree in blossom. The delicate unreal mauve-pink flowers reminded me of a woman's cosmetics and immediately I was taken back to those December days when it had begun to seem that my love for Fay had found a response. I had made one of my stupid mechanical calls on her not expecting – indeed, scarcely hoping – that she would be in. It was just after lunch time on a dim cold day, London's buildings and trees already, it seemed, taking on the uniform grey opaqueness of dusk. I rang and after a while she opened the door, standing for a moment in blue-striped pyjamas. I remember being astonished to find how, without her shoes, I seemed to tower over her; it was a pathetic sign, too, of how little our intimacy had advanced till then. She turned and ran through the sitting-room and kitchen into the tiny bedroom beyond, calling me to follow her. When I got there she was already in bed, the blankets pulled round her neck. The electric fire had made the room stifling.

'I shouldn't have come to the door,' she said, 'I've got the 'flu. Temperature 103.'

I was shocked, as though it were a child who was ill, vulnerable and incapable. 'Have you had the doctor?'

'Yes,' she said miserably. 'I 'phoned him. I hate him really. An awful old man. And someone's got to go for my medicine.'

On a white-painted bentwood chair her clothes were piled confusedly, one nylon trailing to the floor like a wisp of smoke. On the floor by the bed was a copy of *Vogue,* an ancient teddy bear, and a cup gummed to its saucer with old slopped tea. Face powder was scattered among the pots and vials of the dressing-table: a dirty comb lay next to an ashtray full of lipstick-stained cigarette butts. The ottoman at the foot of the bed bore the translation of a Sartre novel and an orange envelope addressed to 'Littlewoods Pools.' All this only made me love her more.

'You want looking after,' I said, with a directness I had never been able to use with her before. She smiled at me mechanically, taking it as though I were really the dominant character. Her face was very pale, her forehead shiny, her hair tangled. I realized for the first time that she was older than I was. I raised her head, plumped and turned the pillow, brought the sheet out and folded it back under her chin as I remembered a kind nursemaid doing for me long ago. Then I took the cup and saucer to the disgusting kitchen and made some lemonade.

When I brought the glass to her she said: 'Sweet of you, Harry.' She raised herself on her elbows and I put the glass to lips that were almost as pale as her face. But instead of drinking her face became distorted. 'What's going to happen to me?' she managed to get out and then fell back on the pillow. Two large tears found their way out of the corners of her screwed-up eyes.

'You've got the influenza-depression,' I said.

She opened her eyes, the pupils brilliant with moisture. 'No, it's more than that. I've been so wretched lying here. I'm quite alone.' She threatened to cry again.

'Cheer up,' I said, purposely ridiculous because I was moved. And it seemed so amazingly fortunate to find underneath the hard, alien chrysalis I had only known till now, this weak, fragile, fluttering creature of my own species.

'It's my life. Growing old and dying,' she said incoherently.

'We'll grow old together.'

'No,' she said. 'No. You can't like me.'

I smoothed back her hair, astonished at first at the audacity of my gesture and then realizing it as a natural part of our new footing. 'I'll go and collect your dope. Where's the old witch-doctor's surgery?'

When I had shut the door of the bedroom behind me with what muscular energy of love had I bounded out of the flat and into the street, seeing happiness stretching indefinitely ahead like the courses at the start of an elaborate banquet! That must have been the twenty-second of December. On Christmas Eve I was still happy. She was not up but was able to share the cold and rather withered chicken I had brought from a delicatessen shop. A bottle of hock gave a curious orgiastic tone to the domestic atmosphere of hot water bottles and aspirin. I had been with her almost continuously for three days, fobbing off Laurence at the office and my father at home with a mythological naval friend returned from foreign waters, and I promised her that I would come again on Christmas Day after the ritualistic family midday dinner at Number 7 which I could not miss on any account. At that she had made a remark which because it showed she was beginning to think about me as an individual pleased me though I did not thoroughly understand it. 'I think you are really a very ordinary person, Harry.' I grinned but did not reply. Of course I was ordinary, if to have strong feelings and a sense of duty and loyalty was to be ordinary. And ordinary, too, in that I understood art without being creative, and could act without action being all my life. But I had never thought of myself as ordinary: and now the deep springs of action and creation had emerged in this terrible form and I had really ceased to be ordinary.

On the night of Christmas Day the thought came to me among the chaos at Number 7 that I had not kept my promise; that she must have been alone all day – worse, perhaps; that I had not even telephoned. A few seconds later the chaos overwhelmed me again and I forgot her. I had never seen her since.

From that day I had thought of her seldom and then only with guilt – guilt not because I had neglected her but because I had been absorbed in her, part of my general guilt. If I had given my father all the love which was rightfully his instead of what was left when Fay had taken her frighteningly gigantic share everything must surely have been different. One memory haunted me – coming home to Number 7 late on the Christmas Eve, feeling gay after drinking most of the hock, and Joe, the family cat walking up to me in the hall. I had stooped automatically to stroke him and then straightened without having touched him, realizing that I couldn't spare any of my love, that I must save all my caresses for Fay.

2

The bus put me down, and I crossed the road and walked up the street, past the antique shop which still displayed the rather rusty suit of armour, past the old-fashioned and desolate shoe shop. Then came the offices: a flight of steps led up to the estate agent's. One climbed them and reached a corridor which ran right through the building. At the end of the corridor a door gave on to a paved courtyard. Round the yard were a brick cottage and some wooden studios. The cottage had been made into two flats: Fay's was the upper. The whole milieu was typical of her: she had always lived, I imagined, in such makeshift places.

I went up the narrow stairs and saw by her door in its metal frame the familiar little card bearing the one word LAVINGTON in violet ink. Everything seemed so quiet and natural, so suggestive of happiness, that I could not imagine why I had never returned nor the obstructions that my mind must have thrown up to keep me from what I most desired – the fear and guilt which had drenched me and made me unclean and unworthy of her. I rang the bell with a sense of pleasure I had never expected to feel again.

As I waited – so long that I knew she could not be in – my desperate situation closed in on me once more and I knew that it was too late for happiness. I looked back down the dark stairs for the Eumenides. But I could not bring myself to go. Away from this place there was no hope for me at all and although happiness was impossible I was breathing, suffering, clinging on to my life with the fundamental, blind instinct of an organism. I pressed the bell again and again, beginning to sweat, feeling time slipping away, and something approaching that was like the determined moment of departure or detonation.

Then, as miraculously as a lock with a key that does not belong to it, the door opened, and Fay stood there just as I had imagined. For long seconds neither of us spoke, and then she said, in a quite normal voice: 'Come in.'

'Are you alone?' I asked.

She nodded. 'I was asleep. Too many gins at lunchtime.'

'I'm awfully sorry to have wakened you,' I said falsely, knowing that interrupted sleep weighed nothing beside my necessity.

The door gave straight on to the sitting-room. Fay shut it behind us and then went to the cigarette box. When she turned round to me I saw that she had conquered whatever annoyance or strangeness she had felt at first. She held out the box, smiling, and said: 'Well, haven't seen you for ages.'

'No one has,' I said in a high voice, looking at the cigarettes. 'I've been ill.'

She arranged the cushions on the divan and reclined. 'Yes, I'd heard you'd been ill. I'm sorry.' It was as though our Christmas episode, even our Swiss relationship, had never happened: we were back on the party-meeting level.

'Who told you?' I asked. I thought: it was Max Callis.

'Oh Laurie or someone. Do sit down, Harry. You look fagged out.'

I sat down. One of us would have to link this meeting with the past, so I said: 'I don't know what you can possibly think of me.' My acting pleased me: it seemed to me that this was precisely the kind of remark the occasion demanded. I had to act, because the sight of her made simply no effect on me. I just had to get from her, quickly but safely, the information I wanted.

She giggled, and then looked at me seriously with her bright eyes. 'Don't let's go into that.'

The serious look drove away my histrionic powers – it struck me like the knowledge of a planned pleasure imparted to a child when his own misconduct has proved it impossible of fulfilment. Suddenly I wanted more than anything to explain that I had loved her and that only the cataclysm of my breakdown had prevented our happiness. But I could not: I could only manage to mumble: 'I've been very ill.'

I hoped even then that she might amplify the shaky short-hand of that confession and divine what had happened to me. It occurred to me fleetingly that it might yet be possible to confide in her, to unload on her sympathy what I had borne alone for so long without any thought that I could lay it down. But she made no comment: perhaps she didn't hear me. She stretched for an ashtray and rattled on about a job she had had and lost, about a visit to Paris and the people and films she had seen there, about her lunch with a business man who had a personal relationship as well as another job to offer her and how she had decided she wanted neither. As so often it seemed to me that her entire conversation and fifth-rate intelligence were things that she used perversely to try to mask her beauty and the real character that should, that must go with it. In a dream I watched the movements of her lips, the hand holding the cigarette and the hand that went gracefully from knee to hair. If she would only will it she could move out of her stupid life into my own. I wished for her, as I had always wished, serious motives, sincere feelings, the capability of being moved and changed by my love. It was true: I had loved her all the time and love, through its negation, had turned to murder.

I said abruptly: 'Did you know that Max Callis was dead?'

I watched closely for her reaction and then was astonished to see how pat the colour rose in her throat and cheeks.

'Yes, I saw it in the newspaper.' She was conscious of her blush and bent her head exaggeratedly as she stabbed out her cigarette. Then she immediately lit another.

'Terrible thing,' I said. I found that I could act again.

'Terrible.' She looked up and met my eyes. 'Suicide,' she said. It was a statement.

'Was that in your newspaper?'

'No, Charles Legge told me. He telephoned.'

'How did he know?'

'I haven't the slightest idea,' she said irritably. 'But what else could it be?'

'You knew Callis quite well, didn't you, Fay?'

She made a gesture. 'Oh, quite *well*,' she said, putting the stress on the unexpected word, as she often did, as though she were trying to give epigrammatic significance to the most trivial remarks. 'I should think you knew him pretty well. You and Laurie published him, didn't you?'

'Did you see him yesterday? Or the day before?'

'Look, Harry,' she said, in a voice which was scarcely hers, 'it wasn't because of me he killed himself.'

'But I wasn't thinking that.'

'Everyone's thinking that.' She reached out and fumbled again in the ashtray. 'We finished days ago. And anyway there was really nothing in it. Nothing.'

'I'm not blaming you, Fay.' I was disturbed at her vehemence. There was no need for her to be upset, no need at all.

'I can see I shall never hear the last of it. First Charles Legge and now you. Is this what you've called about?'

'Fay,' I said, placatingly.

She went on: 'Max was simply a madman, you know. He had no scruples about anything. The only person he ever thought of in his life was himself. He certainly didn't kill himself because of anyone else. If you had ever been with him in one of his black, mad fits. . . .'

While she was speaking I got up and went to the window. It looked over the glass roof of one of the studios. Through an open skylight came the voice of the commercial artist who inhabited the studio – a shrill voice that I remembered from the past, a joke between Fay and me, a voice that swore and laughed by itself at intervals through the day and night. Sparrows sat on the coping of the roof, their droppings running down the glass like whitewash. I watched them hopelessly, seeing everyone in the world in a little separate box of existence, laughing or screaming, without a thought for the other boxes. In her absurd delusion of guilt about Callis, Fay was quite incapable of apprehending reality. I was suddenly seized with a fury of jealousy and peevishness. Why should I have any scruples about breaking down the barriers with which she had surrounded herself? I could, with a word, involve her with me as I had never been able to do in my normality – and let real things into her useless life.

It was strange for me to be standing there, conscious of power over her. 'Fay,' I said, without looking round, 'I know that you think your relations with Callis may have caused his suicide. But it wasn't so.' My voice was clear and emotionless.

'What do you mean?'

'Believe me, it wasn't so.' I turned and saw that she was hanging on my words. 'But perhaps you saw him yesterday or the day before. You probably have clues as to his death – the places you went to, the people you saw, the things he said.'

'But I wasn't with him,' she said. 'And, anyway, you seem to know more about the awful thing than I do. What happened, Harry?'

I tried to be patient with her. 'You see, things may be important that didn't seem important to you then. For instance, where did Callis sleep the night before last? Where was he going to when you left him?'

'Harry,' she broke in, 'didn't you hear me? I haven't seen Max for days.'

It seemed to me that for the first time since I entered the room she was behaving naturally. She was interested in me, in what I had to say. Some emotion had triumphed over the usual artificiality of her manner. Though it was only half smoked she held her cigarette as though she would like to get rid of it. I came and sat next to her on the divan. With a little concentration I could stop my clasped hands on my knees from trembling visibly.

'Please don't lie,' I said.

'I'm not lying,' she said. 'You're behaving very oddly, Harry.'

'I mean, don't bother to lie. You've no need to lie to me. I'm in it, too.'

'Oh for God's sake let's stop talking about Max. He's dead and that's all there is to it. I never really liked him and I'm sure you aren't interested in him.' She stopped and then said: 'What do you mean. You're in it?'

'We must talk about Callis.'

'So that *is* why you called,' she said, puzzled. 'After all these months. I don't understand you, Harry. I don't think I ever did.'

'I'm perfectly easy to understand.' I had to turn away from her: my hands could not be controlled. 'Or I used to be. I still love you.' I got the last words out in a scarcely audible voice.

She laid a practised, neutral hand on my arm and said, non-committally: 'Harry, dear.'

'We must go back to those days before Christmas, cancel everything else,' I muttered. I had meant to act and now found that I couldn't, that I had to mean everything.

'How can we go back?' she said and paused. 'I never knew what really happened at Christmas. Why didn't you come again? I wanted you to come.'

'Oh Fay,' I said and clutched her hand. 'You've got to give me an alibi.' That was it.

After a second she took her hand away. 'An alibi?' There was an edge on her voice. 'What are you talking about?'

'An alibi for yesterday. And the day before. If you weren't with Callis I could have been with you all the time, couldn't I? Slept here at night. You won't mind saying that. We can work out the places we went to. The thing is, it must seem quite normal. That is the best kind of alibi. Nothing too precise. Everything quite normal. Then we can go back, can't we? But I must make you understand about the alibi.'

'What on earth have you done?' she said at last.

'I killed Callis.'

Through the window, into the silence, floated faintly the mad shouting of the artist.

3

She believed me almost immediately. I said: 'It proves I love you. I was jealous of him.' Under the calamity the room seemed to have gone dark. We sat in absorbed communication with our thoughts as though we were wearing headphones. Then I sighed and at the painful sound I felt her body start.

'My God,' I said.

'All the time you never came to me you were jealous.' She was speaking as though we might be overheard.

'I must have been watching you.' I let out the words between hands pressed to my face. 'I *was* watching you. And then the opportunity came.'

'How did you – kill him?'

'I can't remember. I can't remember.' I uncovered my face. 'It's my illness. I can't remember anything. Now you see why we must make an alibi together. You say you weren't with him, so you can have been with me. We can show that I couldn't possibly have got away to kill him.'

'But, Harry, you must know what happened – '

'No. I don't know. But I killed him. I killed him. It's this illness – this breakdown. It happened at Christmas, after one of the other deaths. That's why I couldn't come back to you.'

'Yes, I see, I see,' she said quickly. 'Well, we must work it out.'

'You've got to remember exactly what you did yesterday and the day before.'

'I must think.'

'We'll write it down. We've got to be word perfect.'

'Yes, I see.'

'The police,' I said. 'You won't mind the police, will you? You see, they'll know I was in love with you. They'll find out how I was with you at Christmas. They'll ask you questions, keep on asking you.'

'Yes,' said Fay. 'Yes. The police.'

'Now the day before yesterday. What about that?'

'I can't think,' she said. 'Oh yes. At night I was at the theatre.'

'Which?'

'The what's-its-name – the Haymarket.'

'Were you alone?'

'I was – ' Her voice changed. 'You look all in, Harry.'

'I'm so tired. I don't sleep.'

'Poor Harry.' She rose and touched my hair. 'I'll make some tea. And then we can talk.'

'You must hurry, Fay,' I said fretfully. 'Every second's important. They're bound to find me. Even here. Perhaps especially here.'

'We'll be better with some tea,' she said. 'Much better. There's nothing like a nice cuppa.'

'Hurry. Do hurry.'

She was at the door to the kitchen. 'Shan't be two minutes.'

I was left staring blankly at the cut the ashtray had made on

my hand. I wondered what Mrs Giddy was thinking, eating her
cold pie in the kitchen. Perhaps the police were already inter-
viewing her and she was unwittingly smashing the grounds for
my alibi. Yesterday had been her half day off, but had she gone
out? I could not remember. Yesterday merged with a recession
of others of her half days – bus rides to Richmond, cinemas at
King's Cross, visits to a friend at Brixton. Yet another laborious
task loomed in front of me: getting back to Mrs Giddy, questioning her, establishing her movements, all under the hampering
cloak of innocence. I felt again the inexorable movement of time
past my dream-bogged feet.

But Fay had taken it well. I had one ally at least. I could see
now that it was true that at Christmas she had really started to
care for me. Perhaps it had even been that she had designed her
episode with Callis to bring me back to her. If that was so, how
brilliantly she had succeeded! I saw my murder as a colossal mis-
conception – like some ruinous and bloody attack ordered by a
sincere but incompetent commander. I groaned aloud, and my
nerves jerked me to my feet and sent me pacing round the room.

Everywhere was still. A haze of cigarette smoke hung below
the ceiling, like ectoplasm. A little pink alarm clock ticked
resoundingly: it was 4.20. What on earth was Fay doing? Was it
possible that she could foolishly be buttering bread, cutting slices
of cake? Had she not, after all, believed me: did she think I was
playing some elaborate joke? Perhaps I was back again at the foot
of the mountain with my cruel stone. I started to sweat a little.

The door to the kitchen was shut: I went over and put my ear
against it but could hear nothing. Alarmed, I silently edged it
open. The kitchen was empty. For a few moments I stood, utterly
baffled, hearing the tap tick water into an enamel bowl as loudly
as the clock. A peach-coloured slip and a tea towel were hanging
on a clothes horse. The gas ring under the kettle was unlit. I tiptoed to the bedroom door.

As soon as I had opened it half an inch I heard Fay's voice. It
was pitched very low. It said: 'I think he might be dangerous.' She
paused. 'No. No. Just send someone round here at once. Quickly.
Yes, it's off the Camberwell New Road. Please. Quickly.' It was as
though I had never heard the voice before. A feeling of astonish-

ment swept over me like nausea – astonishment not at her but at myself, as though I were seeing myself through her eyes. It was to me, then, that these clichés could be applied.

I pushed open the door and found myself looking at her across the room. Even in that moment I recognized it as the room in which I had once been happy. Fay was standing by the unmade bed, holding the telephone in her hand, meeting my gaze. The tones of her white sweater were reflected in her face, which was the face of a stranger. She stayed as though she were petrified.

After a few seconds I began very slowly to close the door. I turned the handle carefully so that the tongue of the latch should engage with no sound. I stood alone and shaking in the kitchen. Then I ran into the sitting-room, picked up my hat and coat, and went quickly from the flat. No one prevented me.

Four

I

Nor did the people outside appear to recognize me as a murderer. Nevertheless, I turned up my coat collar, walked rapidly, kept off the main streets. I dared not call a taxi, take a bus, or even run. I thought that every step took me further from danger and yet knew that I carried danger about with me like my shadow.

I could not blame Fay. I was only confirmed in my long-held belief that all I could arouse was fear and repugnance. How cunning people tried to be to hide their feelings about me and how easy it was to find them out! A new access of defiance and hatred enabled me to bear the deep hurt that if I allowed it would well out in self-pity and surrender. At least I had emerged with two threads that might lead to safety: the Corydon and Charles Legge.

When I had walked deep into the regions north of Camberwell Green I went into a public call box. In the stuffy silent cabin my panting was magnified: I was horrified by my face in the mirror behind the telephone. For a moment I gazed at it, appalled at the events which lay behind and before it, wondering at my strength of endurance: then I opened the directory to look for Charles Legge's number.

I believed I knew Legge: I had a memory of a short thin man, youngish but bald, who wore bow ties and phenomenally thick tweed suits. I certainly knew him by reputation. We had once turned down a book of poems of his: he also wrote verse plays which sometimes got produced in churches. He had published a collection of essays on the theme of romanticism in modern poetry, among them one on Max Callis. He worked for the B.B.C.

He was in the book. I dialled the number. While it rang I tried to think what I should say and wondered how much Legge knew and why he should spread the false rumour of suicide. Was it possible that he, too, was plotting against me in some way while pretending to help? The ringing tone ended and a voice said hello.

I pressed the button and tried to control my breathing. I said: 'Is that Charles Legge?'

'No,' said the voice. 'He's out, old boy. This is Gerry.'

'When will he be in?'

'Haven't a clue. Is that Peter?'

'No,' I said. 'This is Laurence. Laurence Sinton.'

'Oh I say,' said the voice, with respect, 'he'll be sorry he missed you. Can I give him a message?'

'No. No, it doesn't matter. Is he at work?'

'No, he's off today.'

'Where does he work? Broadcasting House?'

'No. Bush. Near Eastern Service.'

'Thank you very much,' I said. 'I'll ring him there tomorrow perhaps.'

'Yes, do,' said the voice. 'He'll certainly be sorry he missed you today.'

I put back the receiver. Catching the reflection of my face again I thought: why did I use Laurie's name? There was another reason besides the covering-up of my tracks but it evaded me like a dream on waking.

The door of the box weighed a ton against my exhaustion: for a moment I felt a sharp claustrophobic terror. Then I emerged into the quiet street, where the light was going out of the sky and a lamp flowered yellowly against it. I would have to go to the Corydon when it opened – at six? That was where Fay and Callis had conducted the public part of their affair, where Callis had surely passed his last drunken hours. I had a vision of cleverly interrogating the cloakroom attendant, the barmen, the waiters, the denizens of the place themselves.

Across the way was a café, dingy, with steamed windows through which could faintly be discerned a display of anaemic pastries loaded with shredded coconut, a pile of sandwiches and three tomatoes. I went inside and got a cup of tea from the man standing behind the counter by the hot water geyser. I took it to a marble-topped table away from the two proletarians eating pies and chips.

The thickness of the cup between my lips, the warm sentimentality of the beverage, released a flood of feeling. I thought of Fay and my love as though I were looking at a faint gleam down the dark fearful perspective of a well. It was quite beyond reach, that little dream of happiness. Now I could admit to myself that I had gone to her only with cunning and could excuse her fear and treachery. I myself was afraid – not only of the authorities she had set on to me but still more of the evil inside me.

The café radio started playing the same waltz that I had evoked this morning from my own radio to help create another alibi. I looked up sharply to see if a trap was being set. Through my moist eyes the lamp lighting the café was shattered into needles of brightness. The door of the café opened and an old man entered, his face hidden in the shadow of his hat.

Instantly I remembered those terrors of my childhood. For no reason I would be possessed with panic, as if someone terrifying were present, though the room would be empty. Later, a man used to appear to me abruptly and frighten me so much that I would run away to a remote corner of the house and hide. I could recall precisely the appearance of this figure: it was short, bearded, sallow, with a thick nose – like no one who was known to me in real life. His coming was a secret which I could never share, for he was trying to make me take something shameful. The man came nearer and nearer, insisting that I took it, but at the final moment I was always able to flee.

What was it that I was asked to accept? It seemed incredible that I could not remember. I launched myself back into the life that surrounded that nightmare – Esher Square, where I had been born and always lived; the day nursery at the top of the house which had glass doors through which one could step on to the flat part of the roof; my father – tall, clean-shaven, with the aquiline nose that both Laurence and I had inherited – sometimes coming up to us, his cigar bringing an aura of the adult world. As these clear, sane, happy pictures rose it seemed as though the memory of the phantasmal man could not possibly belong to me. And with them there suddenly came a scrap of dialogue – someone was asking what it was that had to be accepted. 'A sin,' came the reply. 'What kind of sin?' pressed the interrogator. And the answer: 'It was murder.'

At this remembrance I stared stupefied at the tea rocking gently in the cup. Even the events of my remotest past confirmed my guilt. And now I knew what had happened when the short, bearded man had at last ceased to appear. His place had been taken in the hallucination, no less terrifyingly, by the veiled figure of a woman. At last the woman had appeared with her face visible, a brown and emaciated face of death.

Could it be possible that I had only dreamed these symbols of crime and insanity? No, they were too actual for dreams: it seemed to me that they had formed the subject of awful monologues in real rooms, real darkness – carried on through the noise of grown-ups downstairs, lit only by the lights of cars tracking across wall and ceiling. How mysterious and sinister was the past – that faintly known but immense stretch of time when the patterns which adult life merely repeated were formed from naked, savage jealousies and desires. And now that womb of my character had, through my illness, extended itself from childhood as far as yesterday, making my actions as abrupt and unpredictable as those of a tribe brought suddenly into civilization.

The old man brought his cup and cheese roll to the next table. 'Nasty raw wind,' he said to me, as with a visible effort he took off his hat. The face he turned to me was quite unfamiliar.

'Very nasty,' I said.

2

The Corydon Club was in Brewer Street. It had been started in the late twenties. Arnold Bennett had supped there and, in the next decade, James Agate. During the war American patronage had saved it from extinction and now it was almost an institution. Its original flavour of the arts had been diluted by an influx of knowing provincial company directors and newly-prosperous metropolitan professional men, but they still threw out a poet or two every week and there were usually a few beards on the dance floor.

In these post-war years, indeed, there was an atmosphere of the black market about it, but I had quite often used it to lunch authors: there was always whisky in the bar and some abundant but slightly illegal meat dish, like venison, on the menu. The club servants had a manner at once servile and insolent, and one suspected that those at the top of the hierarchy were richer than most of the members. The men's cloakroom at this early hour ought to be empty: I could ask the attendant about Callis – it was only a question of giving him half a crown and finding an excuse. But when I went up to the counter with my hat and coat the attendant was talking to a tall bald young man whom I recognized as the leader of the band that had been playing at the club for about a year.

'You ought to have did them in a double,' the attendant was saying, 'like I told you. Good evening, sir,' he said to me.

The bald young man, who called himself Sonny Frankland, nodded to me: evidently I had a face that had stuck with him. 'So I might,' he said to the attendant, 'but I hadn't the guts. I had such a bad Saturday at the White City.'

I went through the door into the lavatory: perhaps on my way back the time would be more opportune. I washed and combed my hair, and as I took a last look in the mirror I was astonished to find that I had succeeded in creating myself in the likeness of a man who might be seen at the Corydon and remain unremarked. The face was pale, but in the strip lighting the shadows under the eyes would be little more accentuated and violet than anyone else's: the hair was rather long (I had not dared the barber's for over a month) but not too long for the Corydon: the suit, the darker, plain waistcoat, the half-brogue Vandyke suède shoes all belonged impeccably to an era when I had unhesitatingly adopted the standards of general society. The hand that put a cigarette between the serious lips could scarcely be seen to tremble.

In the cloakroom Sonny Frankland still talked to the attendant. They had got on to scandal. 'You watch,' said the attendant. 'You'll see Mary still here when all the rest of the barmaids is gone. Then they go up to his office. Haven't you never seen that bloody big couch he has in there?'

As I passed them I had an inspiration. 'Come and have a drink,' I said to Frankland.

'Never known to refuse,' he said.

We went into the main bar: the chairs and tables were chromium and green leather but someone had recently had the fashionable idea of hanging the walls with a red-striped, mock-Regency paper.

'Do you play the horses?' asked Frankland.

'No,' I said.

He took a sip of his scotch and water. 'Funny thing,' he said. 'I really do all the things I used to be warned against as a boy. Gambling, booze, women and these.' He held up his cigarette between nicotine-badged fingers. 'They ought to have warned me against saving, marriage and milk. Do you think it would have worked?'

He had a public-school accent and the jittery manner of one who never has time thoroughly to recover from his hangovers. In front of his five-piece band he sometimes played the violin, sometimes sang a chorus in a voice still nervous and light but the accent changed to conventional American. As we leaned against the bar the hand without a cigarette worked out some elaborate double stopping on the counter, probably to conceal the whisky shakes.

Because of my invitation he evidently thought he ought to know me. 'D'you know, I simply can't remember your name,' he said.

'Sinton.'

'Ah, yes,' he said. 'Haven't seen you in here for a while, have I?'

'No. I've only come here tonight hoping to see a man called Callis, Max Callis. Do you know him? He's usually in here.'

'Callis,' he said. 'Oldish chap with a stiff leg?'

'No,' I said. 'He's not very old. Squat, rather plump. Gets drunk.'

'Well, the name seems very familiar, but I can't bring the chap to mind. So many of them get drunk. And that reminds me – two whiskies, dear.' He leaned over and squeezed the barmaid's arm.

There are novels and films where the past is reconstructed by the hero's interrogation of casual characters, but real life is otherwise.

'Nice girl, isn't she?' Frankland remarked, as the barmaid went to the bottles at the back of the bar. 'Different from that bag downstairs. But she won't last long. D'you remember Enid? She was nice, too, but she had to go after she tapped Vincent on the nose with a baby tonic. Do you know our Vincent? It's only because I'm usually tight when he comes on the scene that I've stuck him all these months. When he was manager at the Black Prince the band put him out in Curzon Street without his trousers.'

The second whisky dulled the edge of my agitation and I suddenly realized what a source of solace lay at my command.

At last Frankland looked at his watch. 'I must go and get through my first session,' he said. 'I've enjoyed our little drink. See you on the flypaper.' And he went down the stairs that descended from one end of the bar to the floor below. As soon as he had gone I ordered a third whisky and drank it with the mingled relief and guilt with which one consumes a sleeping drug.

The bar had filled up. I kept hoping everyone would go downstairs and eat and I could then get an opportunity to ask the barmaid about Callis. But the bar was a pipe-line that never emptied, and I sat at the counter on one of the stools surrounded maddeningly by high, loud voices, the scent of newly-applied face powder, and snapping cigarette lighters. This and the whisky, like a shot of local anaesthetic, gradually induced a numb despair. Was there nothing for it but to hang on during the long night and wait for the slender chance of getting something out of Legge in the morning? Perhaps I ought to ring him again later in the evening. Certainly I must have another drink.

Then I thought of the bar downstairs: it would be quieter and there was the immoral barmaid to question, a likely contact of Callis's. I moved through the crowd, looking at it in the face, challenging it to challenge me. Nothing happened. At the bottom of the stairs the band could be faintly heard, Sonny Frankland's violin transforming a song of the day into a Bach-like allegro. These corridors and rooms were once the cellars of the building: the walls had been covered with a sort of hard porridge and painted gold but they still retained a damp, oppressive, cellar-like quality. I walked into the bar. It was a smallish square room with a semi-circular counter in the far right-hand corner. At the table in the corresponding left-hand corner, alone and looking straight at me with recognition so that it was impossible to retreat, was Clarence Rimmer. For a moment I had a feeling of fear, as though his presence was a result of his understanding what was behind our lunch together. This feeling immediately gave way to one of irritation: the man was ubiquitous.

Rimmer raised his arm and beckoned with a fat finger. I went over like a schoolboy.

'Hello,' he said, accentuating the last syllable. His shapeless double-breasted suit seemed as familiar as one of my own.

I said hello and tried to grin.

'Are you shadowing me?' he asked facetiously.

Not tonight, I nearly said. 'Extraordinary coincidence,' I actually said. 'Like immediately coming across for a second time a word one doesn't know.'

He said: 'Neither thing being truly extraordinary, because of their respectively restricted worlds. The word, you see, is encountered because – oh, hell, let's not go into that. Have a drink.' He called the waiter.

This was a louder and redder edition of the Rimmer I had lunched with: it was a moment or two before I realized that he was already quite well oiled.

'I'm glad I've met you again, Sinton,' he said, when he had ordered a whisky and a pint of Worthington. 'I'm feeling bloody low and I don't care much about drinking alone. I like you, Sinton.' He held me with his pale watery eye.

I made an embarrassed muttering noise.

'It's all right, Sinton,' he went on. 'I'm strictly heterosexual. No need to get alarmed. What have you been doing with yourself since lunch?'

I said: 'Waiting for the pubs to open again,' but he did not seem to hear. He was lighting a cigarette from the end of the one he was smoking: an operation that demanded his whole effort and concentration.

The drinks arrived and he took a great draught of beer. 'You married?' he asked, wiping his moustache.

'No,' I said.

'Fortunate man,' he said. 'I've been married seven years and now I don't know whether I shall leave my wife or whether she'll leave me. It's a curious state, as you probably know. There's no real reason why we should part. I've no lover and I don't think she has. In fact there's every reason why we should stay together: we find each other attractive, we've got a joint bank account, children, a flat. And yet we have the most exhausting quarrels. That's what I've been doing since lunch.'

'I'm sorry,' I said, inadequately. I felt as though by accident I'd got into a boring entertainment which I couldn't decently leave before the end. I looked covertly round the bar in the ridiculous hope that some cataclysm was brewing which would providentially release me.

Perhaps Rimmer saw my gesture. 'Poor Sinton,' he said. 'There's nothing more agonizing than someone else's matrimonial confessions. But in those matters we all behave like the woman next door, in spite of ourselves. Wait until you are married.'

I smiled and suddenly felt a sympathy and liking for him. 'Let me buy you another drink,' I said, 'and then go home, more or less sober.'

He shook his head. 'It wouldn't work. All right for the errant bank clerk and his missus, but we're too complicated. And I'm low, very low. I need more booze. What about you? Are you waiting for a girl?'

I said: 'No. I'm not waiting for anybody. Same again?'

3

'I suppose we ought to eat,' said Rimmer.

I looked at my watch: it was almost eight. Accelerated by the drinks and Rimmer's monologue the last hour had galloped by. The figures on the dial brought back to me all my desperate situation and the rapid failing of my quest. My cigarette smouldered between fingers that felt thick and my mind ran round on one track: I had had too many whiskies.

'I suppose so,' I said. There seemed nothing else to say.

'Have dinner with me.'

'Thank you,' I said.

We went into the big room where Sonny Frankland and his band were playing and a few couples were gyrating on the dance floor. Around the walls, behind the row of tables, were little ill-lit alcoves where one could eat in reasonable privacy. We went into one of these and sat side by side on the wall seat facing the floor and the great puce-coloured shell affair in front of which the band performed. The music now was slow and melancholy, and Frankland was whispering a chorus through the microphone, his voice hoarse with spirits, his eyes closed in boredom. At a table across the room a girl with lank brown hair and pale face was sitting alone: at my first sight of her I thought she was Fay, and almost got up and fled. I gazed unseeingly at the menu placed in front of me, wondering how I was managing to go through these motions of conventional existence.

'Potted shrimps,' said Rimmer. 'I shall start with potted shrimps.'

'For me, too,' I said.

'And then jugged hare. What about you, Sinton?'

'That would be fine.' I felt the eating of this food lie ahead like the impossible task of a fairy tale. Perhaps Rimmer would be too drunk to notice if I left it. But something – the change of atmosphere or the shrimps – seemed to give him a fresh lease of life. He was as alert and interested as though he had been pouring the beer on the floor instead of down his throat. His 'low' mood had gone.

'One never gets quite enough shrimps,' he said. 'Perhaps one ought to order a double portion.'

My own shrimps lay on my plate like the miraculous draught.

Rimmer laid down his fork. 'Sinton,' he said, not looking at me, 'I never meant to ask you this, but since we've met again so soon I really can't avoid it. Why did you come for me at Sotheby's this morning?'

My heart started to pound and I felt my face growing hot: the emotion of a boy found out in an absurd deceit by a feared master. 'Oh, I forgot, I should have – ' My voice was thick, almost inaudible.

Rimmer said: 'Naturally, my wife told me you had telephoned.'

Of course, as I sat there so close to him, exposed, in a rational milieu, I remembered the incredibly rash telephone call and saw the impossibility of explaining it away. My face was flaming as I stumbled into a rigmarole about the firm and establishing contact with him.

He made it easier for me by interrupting me again. 'I thought myself that that might be the point of it,' he said, 'but you see you never came to it, did you?'

I said: 'I'm afraid since my illness my concentration. . . .'

'I'm rather slow on the uptake with people,' said Rimmer. 'Really I'm only a critic, not a novelist at all. But thinking it over it seems to me that what you wanted to see me for was to pump me about Max Callis.'

'Not at all,' I heard myself saying. 'Of course, I was interested in Callis's death, seeing that he was an author of ours. But there was no other reason beyond curiosity.' The spy, caught with the papers on him, must even then attempt to brazen it out.

'Two jugged hares,' announced the waiter. In an agitated dream of a dozen possibilities I watched him spoon the dark coagulated mess on to my plate. The wine waiter came up with the burgundy. I was abnormally conscious of Rimmer at my side, as immobile, fat and ugly as a piece of Satsuma ware, paying attention not to the food and drink but to my hands, lips, eyes. The nightmare had long since reached the point when the sleeper cannot bear any more and must wake. I dreaded the moment when the waiters would leave us.

It arrived and neither of us had started to eat. It was my move but I had none to make: I sat as stupid as an unwilling child asked to perform. At last Rimmer took up his knife and fork. 'Well, let's see if our choice was wise,' he said. I started to cram the nauseous stuff into my mouth.

My whole body was tense. I thought that perhaps if I refrained from making any large gesture – reaching out for my wine, for example – Rimmer might, by a sort of sympathetic magic, be dissuaded from speaking again of Callis. So I used once to try, equally irrationally, to avert my father from fixing a threatened appointment for me with the dentist. 'You see,' remarked Rimmer, with his mouth full, 'I take size 17 collars, size 6½ shoes. I've a soft body, big chest, bigger stomach. A typical viscerotonic endomorph – easy going, fond of people and fonder still of jugged hare. Now you, my dear Sinton, unfortunately incline to the cerebrotonic ectomorph – you worry too much, you're too good looking, and you can't abandon yourself happily to booze. Eh?'

At last we came to the end of the hare. Rimmer dived into the side pocket of his jacket and pulled out a folded newspaper. 'Have you seen the evening paper, Sinton?'

'No, I haven't,' I said. It was a curious moment to offer me a little reading matter, I thought.

And then the theme returned, with even more devastating effect. 'I couldn't understand,' Rimmer said, 'why you should want information about the circumstances of Callis's suicide. Morbidity? You were too agitated. And if you'd helped to precipitate it or something you would have known already all that I could tell, or at any rate would have wanted the affair to lie fallow. I couldn't make it out, you see.'

Now I could only meet this with silence, working a piece of soft bread into grey compressed shapes.

Rimmer half turned in his place and looked at me. 'There's a piece about it in the evening paper,' he said softly. 'Not much. It ends with one of those sentences that the reader can make anything of he wishes – like a conventional image in an Elizabethan poem. Listen!' He held up the paper: it was folded at the place from which he wanted to read. *'The police have not entirely ruled out the possibility of foul play.'*

Rimmer put the paper back in his pocket: I was glad to see it go. 'If it hadn't been for our encounter this morning,' he said, 'I should have skipped over those words in a most uncritical way. Textual interpretation was never my strong suit. What do they mean, Sinton: do you know?'

It was as though at that moment another person had entered my body and was making it behave in a way I never intended. My hands were in front of my face and through the interstices of my fingers I could see the dim pink-shaded lamp on our table. A melody from the band came strangely to my ears. This alien and unemotional controller of my actions had decided, I heard to my astonishment, to surrender at one reckless blow all my agonizingly held positions.

'I think I killed Callis,' I whispered, in a voice gross with imminent tears.

'You *think?*' said Rimmer. 'What on earth do you mean?'

Then I felt my hands wet: I took them from my eyes and felt blindly for a handkerchief.

Rimmer's hand was on my arm. 'My dear chap,' he said. 'I only want to help you.' When I looked at him his great flat face was composed entirely of sympathy.

'You're too good to me,' I said. 'I'm not worth it. Everything's hopeless.'

He filled up my glass. 'Have a drink,' he said. 'Compose the nerves.'

I sipped the burgundy as though it were tea and I an overwrought girl. Then I said: 'Aren't you frightened of me? Why don't you call the police?'

'I was never less frightened in my life,' he said composedly. 'And I have no intention at the moment of calling the police.'

It seemed astonishing that life could go on after I had confessed to – loosed on the world – something of the terrors that, like corpses, I had lived with horribly for so long. Rimmer even said: 'I want a pudding. What about you?' I managed a smile and shook my head. With wonderment I watched him quickly demolish three jam pancakes.

When the waiter had finally left us with our coffee Rimmer said suddenly: 'Tell me how you killed Max Callis.'

Murder has to be announced at some exact time, in some real place, even over the coffee cups. I made an effort: 'Why should I tell you?'

'No reason.'

'I'll tell you.'

'You've nothing to lose.' Rimmer blew out a cloud of cigarette smoke.

'I'm – I was in love with Fay Lavington.'

'Ah.'

'And jealous of Callis. He was sleeping with her. You knew that. Isn't it obvious why I killed him?'

'I didn't ask *why*,' said Rimmer.

'What do you mean? What do you mean?'

'I want to know how you killed him.'

What should I guess? Poison, strangling? I looked desperately round, feeling my defences once more melting away, dissolving in tears.

'I don't think I can tell you – go through with it,' I muttered.

'You ought to.'

'No. I killed him. Isn't that enough for you? Why should I drag myself through the muck?'

'Take it easy.' Once more the calm heavy hand descended on my arm. 'You see, it's not enough for me.'

It was like some surgical probe that carefully but quite detachedly, pitilessly, searches out a long-feared, long-nursed private pain. 'Oh, hell,' I said, 'oh hell.'

'Well, then?' asked the even voice.

'I can't remember how I killed him. I can't remember anything about it.' All the points of light in the room multiplied, as though some focus behind my eyes had suddenly been changed.

'That's what I thought,' said Rimmer.

4

I found myself telling him the whole thing, as though he were a doctor or a priest. 'Ever since Christmas there've been great gaps in my memory. Sometimes it's the remote past that I can't remember, but more often it's the events of last week or yesterday. Today's Wednesday, isn't it? But for me Monday and Tuesday might never have existed. As you can guess, I've asked myself why these blots should happen, and why they happen in particular places. And there's only one answer, you know – I can't remember because I don't want to remember, because if I did I should be hurt. The blots cover actions of guilt. Sometimes it seems to me, too, that even from things that I can remember my memory omits the really important strand – so that what appear to me to be innocuous happenings may in reality have been ones where I played an evil part. I can't be sure of anything. It's as though all my past consisted of symbols, not events.'

'You make it very clear,' said Rimmer. 'Has it never occurred to you that since you can call up your state of mind, since you still have an obviously rational power of introspection, that your – er – amnesia is capable of an easy cure? Only skin deep, so to speak.'

'Lunatics often know they're lunatics.'

'You take it too hard, my dear chap,' said Rimmer gently.

'But I haven't told you half – half of what I am.' The words would scarcely come out.

'Tell me then.'

'You're so calm about it, Rimmer. As though it weren't real. Doesn't anything shock you?'

'Nothing that comes out of a man's mind,' he said.

I said very rapidly: 'Of course, you are right. These black-outs in my memory would be trivial if there were no other symptoms – cured by a month at Brighton and a course of vitamin tablets. Because I can't remember that I didn't kill Callis doesn't indicate that I killed him in fact.'

'That's what I mean,' he said.

'Rimmer, for the last weeks I've had to lock myself in my flat so that I shouldn't murder anyone. Lock myself in, with a new lock specially fitted and the key given to my housekeeper with a strict injunction not to let me have it. That's what you can tell the police.'

He ground out his cigarette very slowly. 'I see,' he said.

'Before I locked myself up I was tormented by the fear that I might kill passers-by in the street, let alone people I really disliked. I had to give up going to work because my whole days were spent in contriving alibis that I could use in case I went under to these murderous impulses. I used to haunt railway stations, pubs, cinemas, establishing my presence and the time to porters, barmen, cashiers. At regular intervals I used to telephone my flat and give my housekeeper a fictitious account of where I was and what I'd been doing. But the strain became too much. And really the alibis didn't satisfy my conscience. Because I didn't want to kill anyone, Rimmer – my whole being rebelled against the idea of killing. That was the terrible part of it. The madness has infected just a part of my mind. So I incarcerated myself.'

Rimmer silently held out his cigarettes. I took one and he lit it for me.

I said: 'Even in my flat my tortures weren't over. If I glanced out of the window I might see a victim and I would have to watch him until he was out of range of a murderous weapon. If I lost sight of him before that happened I couldn't be sure that I hadn't killed him. The street is within pistol range of my windows. So once again I had to try to make alibis – with chronically limited means: listening to radio programmes, going along to my housekeeper, trying to make the life I was leading look normal. Sometimes I even thought that the fears of the streets were easier to bear than the fears of my self-imprisonment. And again, no lock was really proof against my ingenuity. There was nothing to say that I hadn't broken out of the place in the night, murdered, returned and covered the traces of my breaking out. Because my memory would immediately expunge such adventures. Then the newspapers would arrive – full of accounts of murders committed in London. How could I know that I wasn't guilty of them?'

'And today you saw the report of Callis's death,' Rimmer said.

'I saw the obituary in *The Times*. I daren't at the time look at the report on the news page – it might have brought back the memory of murdering him. I couldn't have borne that. The obituary was enough: I knew immediately that I was responsible. I disliked him, I knew where he lived, where he might eat and drink. He knew me – unsuspecting, he would let me come up to him in a quiet place.'

'Steady,' I heard Rimmer say.

'And then afterwards, when I had brooded on it, I saw that my only chance was to discover the precise circumstances of the murder – and manufacture an alibi to exculpate myself from them. I didn't know where to start. Then I remembered that you lived in the same block as Callis. I thought you would know and tell me what had happened. But all that came out of our fiasco of a lunch was the knowledge of Callis's affair with Fay. A confirmation of my guilt. I went to Fay – another fiasco. When I left her – when I escaped from her – she was on the telephone to the police – or the asylum.'

'You told her?' asked Rimmer.

'I had to have help: I had to. A little while ago I did something for her – nothing much, nursed her through the 'flu. I thought she would remember. . . . Pathetic isn't it? She picked up the phone at once and said: "I've got a homicidal maniac with me".'

'Of course,' said Rimmer, 'they probably won't believe her. I suppose they are bound to check up on you. They'll send a couple of plain clothes men to your flat, and since I gather you haven't been home they'll call again tomorrow.'

'But the police cars, the men on their beats? I got here all right, but there hadn't been time then for a general call. As soon as I walk out. . . . And you, what are you going to do, Rimmer?'

He said: 'Why should they put out a call for a murderer in a matter of suicide?'

'Haven't you understood anything of what I've been telling you?'

'I think I've understood,' he said. 'It's a case of severe obsessional ideas with full insight.'

I stared at him as though it was he who had unfolded his madness and guilt.

He said quickly: 'I'm sure Callis killed himself. It's not him but you we've got to worry about. You are mentally ill – I think you know that yourself. But you're no more a homicidal maniac than – than Sonny Frankland or whatever his ridiculous name is.'

The sickly-sweet amplified tones of the violin encompassed a slow melody of extraordinary banality. Underneath, the dancers' shuffling added an irregular ground-bass. The gravely sick man

hears through his pain the specialist say: 'The prognosis is not
entirely hopeless,' and the character of his existence is utterly
changed. I felt a dim but precise excitement, as of a pleasure
promised far in the future.

Rimmer said: 'Don't you see it? It's all so obvious, my dear
chap. There isn't a single factual clue connecting you with Max
Callis's death, or anyone else's. Jealousy? One could make a list
of five husbands who had reason to be jealous of him – he had
his foot in umpteen beds. They're daggers of the mind that you
see. And then the psychological character of your obsessions.
I've only got the ramshackle psycho-analytical knowledge of
a literary critic, but it seems absolutely clear to me that this is
merely a temporary breakdown. If you were schizophrenic, for
example, how could you possess the lucid consciousness you
have of your mental processes? And if you were truly insane your
morality would have gone – and believe me you strike me as the
most moral young man I've ever met.'

He took a gulp of his wine. I stood within a measurable dis-
tance of believing in his incredible words.

'The sooner you get on a psychiatrist's couch the better. That's
my firm advice to you,' he said, arranging his moustache.

Was that all there was to it? A weekly appointment, the
writing-out of a cheque?

'This state of yours,' Rimmer went on, 'must have had a pre-
cipitating cause. Some emotional upset – a violent one. Can you
remember that?'

I felt the tears at the back of my eyes. Of course: sometimes
I could remember nothing else. Every night I lived through it all
again. 'Yes,' I said. 'I remember how it started.'

'You see?' he said.

'It was at Christmas, when Fay was in bed with the 'flu. I was
looking after her, spending whole days with her, staying away
from work and home. That was right up to Christmas Eve. I
promised her that I'd go back on Christmas Day after lunch. But I
never went – and I never saw her again until today.' It was almost,
after all, easy to say.

5

And in the end I told Rimmer, in a voice that poured out of me as though it were being produced by mechanical means, the story of those Christmas days, keeping almost nothing back, turning myself emotionally inside out without shame. He sat smoking and drinking, occasionally nodding: I felt as though I had always known him or, rather, that I had always desired to know him – the competent, un-shockable, omniscient figure who nevertheless was capable of engaging my love.

My father (I told him) was Gifford Sinton, of Eldridge and Sinton, the chartered accountants. My mother died when I was very young. I have always thought of my father as over-strict and yet looking back at this moment I see that though he was dogmatic about small things, such as punctuality and tidiness, in larger affairs he was dominated by his love for us. When my brother Laurence came down from Oxford a few years before the war he announced his intention of going into publishing instead of being articled in the firm. Though this must have been a blow to my father he raised no objections – beyond questioning my brother exhaustively about the economics of the thing and the reasons for his choice – and immediately used his influence to put Laurence with Cuffs to learn the business. Myself, I went straight from Oxford into the Navy: at that time the war had already begun.

When I was released from service at the end of 1945, I, too, decided against accountancy. By then Laurence was anxious to start publishing on his own, so I joined him, my father putting up the capital and forming the company. It was a highbrow affair, as you know. Both Laurence and I had an allowance from my father: the publishing company was never intended, during its first years at any rate, to make profits. I was still living at the family house in Esher Square, but for quite a long time Laurence had had a flat of his own. He had left Esher Square while I was in the Navy: I don't remember that there was any fracas between him and my father – I imagine that he simply wanted more independence in his private life.

I think my father had always overworked. During his twenties and thirties he had been responsible for the growth of Eldridge and Sinton into one of the leading firms: as well as the London practice there were branches to look after, public utility companies in South America and trading companies in the Far East. Between the wars, when younger partners came into the firm, my father went into public life – he was on hospital and polytechnic boards, and governor of his old school, a justice of the peace, and twice stood unsuccessfully for Parliament in the Liberal interest. He had two hundred acres in Hampshire where his hobby was to breed Guernseys. But this and some of his other burdens were shed just before the war. Returning from Glasgow on the train after a battle with the recalcitrant and incompetent board of a shipbuilding company, he was found unconscious in a lavatory with a perforated duodenum.

After this he permitted himself to admit to his indifferent health, and though he usually treated his peptic weakness with the contempt he always showed for other forms of weakness, he undertook regular spells of dieting and rest with a bad grace but a stubborn determination to die eventually through a more dignified cause than an indifferent digestion. I remember many dinners at Esher Square after the war when he would prop the evening paper in front of his steamed fish so that he should see as little as possible of what I was eating. On steamed fish nights also he eschewed his after-dinner cigar. He would watch me smoke my cigarette and say: 'I wish I liked those things.' And I would say: 'But father, they'd be just as bad for you as cigars.' 'I'm not convinced about that.' And then perhaps he would prowl to the mirror and gaze at himself. 'I don't look like an ulcer patient,' he used to say. 'That's the extraordinary thing. Perhaps those damned doctors are wrong. Perhaps I need *more* cigars and beefsteaks.'

Last Christmas Day dinner was at midday, as I had always remembered it being. Laurence came in the morning and we all exchanged presents. The drinks arrived: Laurence and I had sherry and we saw my father with a glass containing a purplish liquid. Laurence said: 'What on earth are you drinking, father?' 'Dubonnet,' replied my father. 'I've been sold on the advertisements.' Laurence said: 'My dear father, it's the liver not the stomach it doesn't affect.' 'Well, I've got to drink something at Christmas time. I was persuaded into drinking gin and tonic at the club last night. That's a beverage that tastes as though it ought to do you good but it's very deceitful. I think it upset me a little. I've felt squeamish ever since. And I must make a decent show at dinner – Harrison has gone to enormous trouble.'

My father did heroically with the turtle soup, the sole, the turkey, the plum pudding; and he drank a glass of champagne. At the end of it he said: 'I think I shan't offend anyone if I give the mince pies a miss. But you boys must eat one.' Coffee was always served in the sitting-room: he told Baker to put his antacid powder on the tray with it. When we went upstairs and helped ourselves to coffee my father preceded his with a tumbler of alkali and water. When I saw him with a glass of brandy as well, I said: 'What a mixture! You'll pay for this!' My father said: 'They must fight it out. I shall try to ignore the battle.'

As we sat there I was wondering all the time when I could with decency slip away to Fay. I was hoping that Laurence had some engagement and would make the first move. But he sipped his coffee and brandy very leisurely and then said: 'What about a hundred up?' 'I couldn't possibly play until I've given my digestive processes some sort of chance,' my father said. 'Harry will give you a game.' So Laurence and I went to the billiards room, leaving my father in his usual chair in front of the fire, rather somnolent.

I was on edge during the game. The time was slipping by, Fay would be wondering what had become of me. Laurence played badly – he never had an eye for any games: I gave him fifty as I always did but in my exasperation played almost as badly. The game seemed interminable, but Laurence at last finished it with a break of fifteen which pleased him very much. I left him continuing it, in an effort to beat his own personal record, and went to see if I could make reasonable adieus to my father.

He was still in his chair, so still that I thought he had dozed off. But when I went nearer to him I saw that his eyes were open. He said: 'I'm afraid I was very foolish to indulge in so much food and drink, Harry. I feel decidedly queer. Do you think you could

get me another draught of my powder?' He was very pale. I got
some water and mixed the powder with it, but when I made to
hand the tumbler to him he waved it away and his head fell back
on the chair. 'Do you know, Harry, I think I'm going to faint.'
I felt helpless. I took his hand and said: 'What can I do, father?'
His eyes were closed: he shook his head feebly. Then he said: 'It's
passing off a little, I think.'

I asked him if I should ring for Baker so that he could be
helped to a sofa. He said no, but he thought he *would* lie down.
He rose and I took his arm. On the way to the sofa I felt his legs
give way under him and I could do nothing but let him sink to the
floor. I managed to hold him in a sitting posture and tried to let
his head go forward as I had heard should happen to the subject
of a fainting fit. His breathing was stertorous, alarming. I looked
round desperately, hoping that someone would come in the
room. It was unspeakably strange and terrifying to be grasping
my father's limp shoulders, to be supporting the lean, livid face
which despite his affection he had seemed always to hold aloof
from us.

A few moments later Laurence found us in this intimate but
ridiculous embrace. I said, unnecessarily, 'Father's ill.' We got
him on to the sofa and there he began to breathe more normally.
'I shall send for Riddell,' Laurence said, with his usual decision.
'Do you know the number, Harry?' My father's eyes were half
open: I think he heard, but offered no comment. Laurence went
to the study telephone. My father said: 'I'm spoiling your Christmas Day.' I said: 'Nonsense, father. Now don't try to talk.' He
said: 'I'm afraid I feel as I did that day on the train. I hope I haven't
perforated again.' 'I hope so,' I said fervently but inadequately.
'Do you think your powder would do you good now?' 'No,' he
said. 'I don't think I can manage it.'

I was kneeling by the sofa, my hand laid over my father's.
Quite suddenly he gave a great retching sound, raised his head a
little, and vomited. My nausea was almost cancelled by pity. With
my handkerchief I was wiping my father's mouth and the moisture that was running from his eyes when Laurence returned.
Laurence said: 'Riddell's coming right away. Good Lord, what's
happened?' 'Get Baker to fetch some warm water and some

towels,' I said. As he went over to the bell Laurence said: 'It was really most injudicious of father to tackle that dinner.'

The vomiting seemed to bring relief. When we had cleaned him up, and propped his head and shoulders on some cushions, a little colour came into his face. He said: 'Did I hear Laurence say that he'd sent for that old woman Riddell?' There was something of his former tone in his voice. I even began to wonder if we had been too hasty: my father detested unnecessary fuss about his own affairs. But Laurence said: 'Yes, father' in a manner even more authoritative, and my father closed his eyes with a sigh. 'You'll have ruined his siesta,' he said.

When Riddell arrived it seemed to me that he had been doing himself very well, even for Christmas Day. He bounced in, the voice excessively loud and cheerful. He was a little red-faced man with white hair growing out of his ears, and he had doctored the family for as long as I could remember. He thought he was a better man than I'm sure he was: my father was always rather irascible with him, though they played bridge together at the club. Laurence had gone downstairs to meet him and had evidently told him of my father's indulgence at dinner time.

'Well, what's all this, Gifford?' said Riddell, as he came in at the door. 'I expect to be called out on Christmas Day to schoolboys but not to old men who should know better.' He stood over my father. 'Pain in the tummy?' he asked. 'A slight one,' said my father. 'Tut, tut,' said Riddell. Laurence and I went out while Riddell examined my father: a few minutes later he joined us.

'Get him to bed,' he said, 'with a hot bottle for his stomach.' He handed Laurence a prescription slip. 'Can you get this made up?' Laurence said: 'I'll go to the Boots in the Circus.'

'He's not perforated himself, has he, doctor?' I asked. 'Goodness, no,' said Riddell. 'The abdomen's a little tender, but what can you expect? There was nothing unusual about the vomited matters, was there?' 'No,' I said. 'I'll call back before dinner. Or maybe just after,' said Riddell, and ran downstairs rather erratically and let himself out.

Baker and I took father to his room while Laurence went in his car to the chemist's. We had got my father half undressed when he said: 'I think I must go along the corridor.' It was our old family euphemism for the W.C. I asked him nervously if I should come with him. He said: 'Of course not.' Nevertheless I waited for him outside the door. The minutes began to add up. At last, breaking through the weight of a lifetime's taboos I called 'Father' and, when there was no answer, turned the handle of the door.

He had not locked it: perhaps he had suspected that the intimacies of his life might have to be uncovered. He was lying on the floor, unconscious in his sickness and ordure. I must confess that instinctively I retreated from the sight, calling 'Baker, Baker' as perhaps I had called years ago in the dark. Helping him back to his bedroom, the aged look of his thin neck, revealed by the collarless shirt, etched itself forever on my memory.

Laurence's return restored my sanity a little. I had had several impulses – to send again for Riddell, to send for someone else more competent, even to go out of the house, away from the embarrassment of my father's suffering. Laurence said: 'We'll see how he responds to Riddell's physic. Of course, he has thoroughly upset himself – we must expect a good deal of sickness and diarrhoea.' It all seemed reasonable – and certainly, in bed, my father once more perked up a little. He kept the medicine down, he admitted that the hot bottles were comforting to his stomach.

Just after six he vomited again, but less copiously. There were some threads of blood. He said, when the violent gasping which succeeded the sickness had subsided: 'What time did Riddell say he was coming again?' I think those words, almost more than anything else, told me how ill my father felt. But when Riddell arrived, close on eight o'clock, my father was again in better shape. 'A very severe bilious attack,' said Riddell cheerfully, when I pressed him for a diagnosis. 'The blood? My dear boy, when the patient strains like that he often ruptures a tiny blood vessel.' It was clear that for him the evening's wining had already started. 'I'm at home tonight – ring me if you need me,' he said. 'But in any case I shall come round first thing in the morning. You can give the patient some glucose water, if he'll take it. That'll help him to keep his strength.' Obviously Riddell had built up his practice on some good quality – perhaps it was the capacity to inspire confidence. Even a bilious attack, I told myself when he had gone, must seem alarming in a peptic ulcer subject: there was really no reason to think Riddell mistaken.

It was nearly nine o'clock before Laurence and I were sitting down to dinner. We had left Baker with my father: he valeted him as well as buttled and was probably the best person in the house for the job. During dinner Laurence announced that he would stay the night: I felt some of the burden pass to him and was enormously relieved.

When we went to the bedroom afterwards Baker told us that my father had been sick again. But at the moment he was sleeping – peacefully, it seemed to me. Baker had had a fire lit in the room: on the marble-topped console table near the bed he had arranged the medicine, the tumblers, the glucose drink. I saw that my father's bedside book was *Old Mortality* and for some reason it seemed pathetic that he should last night have been re-reading Scott and tonight lie here ill, with the implements and ritual of illness round him. 'Of course,' said Laurence, 'someone must be with him all night. We'll take turns – what do you call it? Watch and watch about.' Laurence often used to drag naval terms into his conversation with me, as though there were something witty in it. 'If Baker will go to bed now he'll be able to relieve us early in the morning. Though by then it may very well not be necessary – I think the worst's over.'

Laurence took the first turn. I went to my room, thinking that I shouldn't be able to sleep. I lay in the dark, gazing out, seeing that sordid and moving image on the lavatory floor. And then the next thing I knew was that the electric light was breaking through my sleep and Laurence was at my side. 'Sorry to wake you so soon, Harry. I've been rather worried. I wanted to know what you thought.' The clock said twenty past two. A great depression came over me. I got my dressing-gown and we went along, Laurence telling me that father had been very sick again, but was now asleep. 'If he can sleep, that's a good sign surely,' I said. I wanted above all for things to be less black.

I dared hardly break the barrier of fear that guarded my father's room, but at last I opened my senses to the tableau illuminated by the bedside light – a patch of yellowness surrounded by the dark forms of furniture and curtains, like some Victorian story painting, and my father's head in the middle of it, a towel under the chin, the eyes closed, the jaw slightly dropped. I was shocked by the change that had come over the features – they were thinner, darker, less informed by any quality of mind. I realized that previously my father had scarcely looked ill at all, and I wished with all my soul that we could go back to the early evening which now by comparison seemed a happy and auspicious time.

While Laurence and I discussed whether we should get Riddell up at this unearthly hour my father rallied again. He opened his eyes and asked for a drink. It was surprising to me to find his voice still strong, his manner calm. Once more I wondered if we were worrying unduly. When he had had his drink father said: 'Laurence get to bed,' and, such was the force of habit, Laurence went with little more ado. I sat in the easy chair which Laurence had pulled up to the bedside.

Father said: 'I suppose you don't remember that Christmas when I had measles.'

'Measles?' It seemed astonishing to me that we should talk about ordinary subjects. 'No, I don't.'

'You were very small,' he said. 'You should have had them by any reasonable operation of nature, not I. They're very painful in an adult. It quite ruined our Christmas.'

'I wish you wouldn't keep worrying about Christmas being spoilt,' I said. 'All we want is to see you better.'

'Dear Harry,' he said. 'Always conscientious.'

I was very touched: I never remembered him saying anything so openly affectionate.

'How are you feeling, really?' I asked.

'My stomach is in an extraordinary mess,' he said. 'And this sickness seems to have exhausted me. I do hope you boys haven't inherited my gastric apparatus.'

We talked like this at intervals through the rest of the night: I had never felt so close to him – it was almost as though he were my contemporary. Sometimes he fell asleep, but very restlessly, shifting about uneasily under the bedclothes. When he moaned my heart beat violently. Once I went to the window and parted the curtains and saw the snow falling through the lamplight in the square. Shortly before six the admirable Baker came in with a cup of tea for me and persuaded me to go back to bed.

I woke again at nine, with a guilty sense of escape from responsibility. But despite my guilt I went straight down to the dining-room. Laurence had finished his breakfast and was smoking a cigarette. Riddell was standing with his back to the fire, drinking coffee. 'We must have a nurse,' he was saying, 'though it's going to be the devil's own job to get one on Boxing Day. I'll see what I can do.' 'How is he this morning?' I asked. Riddell blew out his scarlet cheeks. 'He doesn't tell me,' he said. 'Well, must be off. Thank you for coffee.'

Laurence saw him out. When he came back I said: 'Don't you think we ought to have a second opinion? It's obviously more than a bilious attack – even a severe one.'

Laurence had the serious look that I knew so well. 'Riddell's talking about gastro-enteritis now,' he said. 'I think he's quite capable, you know, for a thing of this sort. It's clearly got to take its course. Nursing is the important thing, and he's going to lay that on.'

'Is there anyone with father?' I asked.

'Giddy's there now,' said Laurence.

'Giddy? Father hates the sight of her. I'll go up.'

'What about breakfast?'

'I don't want any,' I said.

'You ought to have some,' Laurence said.

'I couldn't get it down.'

Mrs Giddy was a very old servant, in her element at times of crisis, and most apt to presume on her length of service. I got rid of her, and stayed with father until Laurence made me go down for lunch.

But there's no need for me to tell you this hour by hour. During the afternoon the snow stopped: its pall deadened the already moribund world of a London square on the day after Christmas. And as the day wore on it became clear beyond all hope that my father was very ill. The sickness continued – painful heavings without result that it was anguish to watch – and now it was not followed by those better periods that before had renewed our hopes. In the evening the nurse arrived and, shortly afterwards, Riddell. Riddell now talked ominously about my father's heart: after all, he said ebulliently, he's sixty-seven. 'I happen to know,' he added, in the smugness of health, 'because he's exactly my own age.' He started father on some injections.

The nurse, of course, turned us out of the sick room: she was to be on duty through the night. As I wandered over the house after dinner, everywhere save in that fatal place, it seemed to me that I was being relieved from responsibility against my deserts, that by not being with father continuously, to bear mentally his physical pain, I was betraying him. Before bedtime Laurence and I went in to see him. With a number of little touches Nurse Collins had given the room the cold efficiency and order that alone enables a profession to be made of looking after the ill – that at once negates suffering and attempts to make it bearable. Her little powder-blue travelling clock ticked on the console table by a temperature chart: *Old Mortality* had given way to *The Sittaford Mystery*.

My father opened his eyes and smiled at us. Laurence made some would-be cheerful remark, but father did not reply, only kept on his smile. Then he coughed, and while it continued we talked of trivialities to Nurse Collins. The cough had started earlier in the day – a patient, persistent, unavailing attempt to bring, it seemed, some obstruction up from the lower throat. The quiet sound haunted me all night.

Another nurse, a day nurse, arrived in the morning. Riddell, after he had seen his patient, said to us: 'He's a stoic. I wish his heart were stronger.' Laurence went to the office for a couple of hours, but I had no thought save of staying in the house. I had slept badly and felt exhausted. Why, I kept asking myself, had we not taken more care of father, as it seemed to me then we could so easily have done? Several times I went to my father's door, sometimes hearing the chink of metal on glass or the day nurse humming a song, and sometimes the coughing.

At breakfast on the morning of the fourth day Laurence tried to persuade me to go to work, but I could not bring myself to leave the house. I saw father in the morning – a painful visit. His face above the bed-clothes had a colour that did not belong to humanity. It was freezing outside and the snow still blurred the trees in the square. Somehow the time passed. Meals were served, the machine of the house revolved, but all was tinctured by what went on in the upstairs room. And then the whole character of the day changed. Riddell said to us on his way out after his evening visit: 'Well, he's a good deal better tonight. The tenesmus has been less severe.' He bustled off and Laurence and I were left looking at each other, trying to hide our smiles, afraid almost to move so as not to ruin our luck. Father was asleep when we looked in after dinner: Nurse Collins was reading her book; it seemed true that the awful anxiety was about to be lifted. Laurence said he would nevertheless stay the night again, and we played billiards and drank some scotch.

The following morning as I was having my bath Laurence came knocking at the door. He said: 'Harry, the nurse thinks we ought to go in to father. He's much worse.' I saw the wrist shaking of the hand that had grasped the side of the bath: the old infinitely sad and hopeless feeling returned to my stomach. Laurence was waiting for me outside the bathroom. As soon as we reached my father's door we heard his breathing: it was as though the matter he had so long been trying to cough up he had at last been successful in bringing to the junction of his throat and nasal passage, and through which his breath had now laboriously to pass. The face was dark, the old hands rested unmoving on the eiderdown and there was no struggle – though it sounded painful, the breathing seemed automatic, not a function at all of the exhausted body. There was the unplaceable smell in the room as there had been the whole time.

'I'm afraid he's going,' said the nurse.

'Oh, no,' I said.

Laurence took my forearm with his hand. 'I've sent for Riddell,' he said.

'Why is he so long?' I said. 'Can't we do anything?'

The snoring went on. I saw that my father's eyes were open and for the first time in my life noticed that they were the clearest light grey. Laurence went to the other side of the bed to be nearer father and stood with clasped hands as though he were in church.

Then the frightful noise stopped. I looked at Laurence half

expecting him to smile and say that the crisis had miraculously passed. But instead he said: 'He's dead, Harry,' and started to come back towards me.

I heard my father sigh. 'No,' I said, 'No, he's not.'

The nurse said in her Scottish tones: 'It's the air, just.'

Then I turned to my father: his jaw had dropped too far and he was looking forward at an indefinable point.

6

Rimmer lit yet another cigarette.

'I didn't even remember Fay until weeks later,' I said. 'And then only because I was thinking why it was father had to go to the club on Christmas Eve of all nights and drink that gin. I realized that the reason was that I had deserted him for Fay.'

'It's classically clear,' said Rimmer. 'I think you see that yourself, don't you? The painful death and your feelings of guilt – all that has been transferred to other people, strangers in the street. . . . Max Callis.'

The after-theatre crowd had now invaded the room: a pall of smoke like the aftermath of nuclear fission hung beneath the low ceiling. The drink had made my head ache; I was hoarse with talking, and my mind was full of the images of my father's death. But I did indeed see what Rimmer was driving at. Perhaps if I could have a quiet period of grace I could think it all out.

Rimmer went on: 'What still isn't explained, of course, is why your obsession is so complete: why as an intelligent adult you should delude yourself into thinking yourself a murderer – simply because of the death of your father. After all, when all of us are men our parents die, often painfully, and we must suffer the experience, readjust ourselves to the loss, and remain the same men we were before.'

'Yes,' I said eagerly. I watched Rimmer as though at last he were preparing to hand me the secret of happiness, of how to live.

'My dear chap,' he smiled, 'I'm only a friend, not a Freud. I want to help you, but you need more than a boozy evening in the Corydon.'

I looked down at the table, at the ashtray like a mouth full of bad teeth, and the dregs of wine already drying in the glasses. All the same, merely to put the question opened up vistas in my mind that for months had been impenetrable.

'You see,' Rimmer said, 'there is something else, something you haven't told me about. Something that you *really* don't remember.'

'Something else?' I repeated.

'Some other trauma of the past – as hurting and revolutionary as your father's death,' Rimmer said. 'Do you know those shrubs that grow an almond-shaped leaf bud? This bud is composed of two leaves, their edges together. If you nip it from the bush and open the two leaves you find inside them two similar but smaller leaves, growing at ninety degrees to the outer leaves. And then the inner leaves can be opened to disclose two more leaves growing at ninety degrees to *them*. And so on to the tiniest leaves in the heart of the bud – which human fingers are too crude to open. Forgive this corny and elementary symbolism. But the psychological events of one's life are like those sets of leaves. Involuntarily we make similar patterns – our life with the mother is repeated in our life with the wife, for instance. However far you go back you only encounter the same shapes from different angles. That's what I mean when I say that buried in your past is a succession of events that echo the guilty emotions that rose from the last event, the last trauma – your father's illness. And only a trick cyclist can dig them out – and make you live over the healthy solution of them.'

'I see,' I said, fighting to keep down, as it were a most deadly nausea, the feeling of horror that had been mounting inside me all the time he had been speaking.

'And only then,' Rimmer continued, 'will you see without the slightest doubt that your murder of Callis was committed merely in fantasy.'

There was no need for a psychoanalyst. At last – and it had been so obvious that it had hidden itself from me by its glaring presence – I understood without further question why I had put myself away as a lunatic, why my mind refused to remember, why the days at Christmas had been filled with more than their actual horror. My father's death had not been natural. He had been poisoned. And the murderer – the act forgotten, buried beneath delusion – was . . . myself.

A diminutive figure came to our table, patted Rimmer on the back, and said in a Lancashire voice: 'Hello, Clarence. How's tricks?'

'Hello, Ernest,' said Rimmer. 'What have you been doing with yourself?'

'Ah've just been to see t' Chekhov play at the Arts,' said this figure. 'What a luvly bit of work, Clarence. Have you seen it?'

'No,' said Rimmer, in a depressed tone.

'You must see it. Shows us all up. Luvly craftsmanship. And it's funny, Clarence, really funny. That's where you highbrows make the mistake – Chekhov's a comical playwright, not a sad one.'

Rimmer said: 'Do you know Harry Sinton, Ernest? This is Ernest Schofield, Sinton.'

Of course I knew the name, he was a popular novelist who imagined that his novels had greater virtues than their popularity, a professional plain man, a studied optimist. He should have been big, fat and hearty, but here he was with pale nondescript features and almost a midget. He said: 'Glad to meet you. You're a publisher aren't you, Sinton?'

I said I was.

'I know your brother,' said Ernest Schofield. 'Now that's a chap I respect. Does nowt but the best and yet makes money out of it.'

'Harry's in the firm, too, you know,' said Rimmer, looking at me and surreptitiously raising his eyes in derision at our companion.

'Of course he is,' said Schofield. 'And made fifty for the Publishers against the Authors last year if I remember right. I was there.'

'It's becoming very fashionable for writers to take an interest in cricket,' said Rimmer. 'It proves they don't live in ivory towers.'

'I've always been interested in cricket,' said Schofield. 'And I don't need that to prove I don't live in any ivory tower. But then I'm only a teller of tales.'

'Sit down here for a few minutes,' I said to Schofield. 'I've got to pay a call.'

'Well, just for a little while,' he said. 'I've left Mrs Schofield over there.'

Perhaps I was not acting my nonchalance as well as I thought: as I sidestepped from behind the table I saw Rimmer watching me with the covert readiness to pounce with which one watches a young child. Still, how could he stop me? I walked round the edge of the dance floor very slowly, assuming a great interest in the dancers, feeling Rimmer's eyes on me. I tried to find reassurance by telling myself that he had no reason to know that my whole life had, during the last ten minutes, suffered a profound metamorphosis.

But not until I had got my hat and coat, exchanged false good nights with the attendant, and emerged alone into the streets of Soho did the complete realization of that change grip me, constrict my heart, set my legs on a tremulous wandering voyage, and fill my brain with the staggering enormity of my crime. It was that characteristic and unmistakable time in the West End when normal entertainments have ended and the streets are full of taxis and cars with those who have decided to go home, while the rest seem prepared to wait until the lights go out, and walk rather slowly past the vendors of pornographic magazines and roast chestnuts, and the tube entrances are littered with paper and one begins to notice the eccentric outcasts enveloped in rags, huddled in doorways, and drunken groups appropriating as their disputatious or amatory ground whole sections of side streets.

I walked north, and in Soho Square stepped into a call box and dialled my own number. After a little time I heard Mrs Giddy say hello.

'Hello, Giddy,' I said. 'Did I get you out of bed?'

'No, Mr Harry, I've been waiting up for you.'

'I'm sorry, Giddy. I should have called you before. I shan't be home tonight. My friend is no better and I'm going to stay with him.'

'Oh, Mr Harry.'

'Yes, Giddy?'

'There were two persons – two men – called for you late this afternoon. They wanted very particularly to know where you

were. You'd better tell me in case they come back. It seemed to
be urgent.'

'I know what they wanted, Giddy. It's not important.'

'Won't you leave your number, Mr Harry?'

'I shan't be in to breakfast, of course, Giddy. I'll try to ring you
again in the morning.'

'Are you feeling all right, Mr Harry?'

'Fine, Giddy.' I put back the receiver. I had a clear image of the
entrance to my flat: they would leave it free, naturally, but have
a man in the doorway of the tailor's shop which was separated
by the width of a plate glass window from the doorway to the
offices and flat. There might be another man somewhere: perhaps on the basement stairs where they came up round the lift
shaft to the ground floor. I rapidly put night between myself and
the call box.

7

One of my recurring private fears had for a long time been that I
should contract an incurable and agonizing malady. Sometimes
before I went to sleep I would try to work out what I should do
if the fear became actuality, how I could cheat the lingering, the
unbearable illness. In my imagination I have locked the bathroom door and climbed into the bath with a razor blade: taken a
train to the coast and swum out to sea: bought, at different chem-
ists, a grotesque number of aspirins: found a hotel room with a
gas fire. Now, as I crossed Tottenham Court Road, high up its
length, I found myself acting out the day dream in reality and it
seemed more fantastic than ever it had done in my imagination.

At this moment Rimmer would have realized that I had done
a bunk. Perhaps he had searched the lavatories to see if I were ill.
What action would he take, if any? Even if Rimmer recanted his
idea that my murder was fantasy he could only lead the police as
far as the Corydon: after that the trail was stone dead. My crowd
of emotions admitted yet another – I felt sorry for Rimmer.

I found my hotel in one of the canyon-like streets towards
Euston. It spread across two terrace houses and over the front

door its name was picked out in neon tubing – London House Hotel. Behind the reception desk a weak-faced man in a grey alpaca jacket was writing out bills. I asked him if he had a room.

'Certainly, sir,' he said. 'Just for yourself would it be?'

I knew I had picked wisely. 'Yes,' I said. 'I'm afraid I haven't any luggage. I've been in London for the day on business and now I've missed my connexions.'

'That's all right, sir. Will you just sign the book?'

I took up the pen and put: 'Ernest Schofield. 31 Smith Street, Leigh, Lancs.' Under the nationality column I wrote, more accurately: 'British.'

'Perhaps you wouldn't mind paying in advance, sir.' He was weak but knew the drill.

'Of course,' I said.

'Single room and breakfast. It's just a pound.'

I handed him the note and he took a key from the board at his back. 'Number 10, sir. It's just up the stairs and at the end of the corridor.'

He returned to his bills and I went up the staircase. In the corridor I passed an American sergeant with his tie knot pulled down and his collar unbuttoned. He nodded. The floor of the corridor was covered with linoleum and a dim light from the ceiling left shadows in the corners. Everything had taken on a spectral quality: I could not believe that here my life must end. Before I reached my room I called in a lavatory. There was a torn sheet from the *Daily Mirror* on the floor and a condom floating in the pan.

At length I had to open the door of Number 10. There was just enough space to get by the bed to the furniture at the window. Beyond the foot of the bed, on the same wall, was a gas fire. Involuntarily I put my hand in my pocket and fingered the shillings I had already made sure I possessed. The room was cold: I drew the curtains but did not light the fire. Still in my overcoat I sat in the sole chair, a dilapidated wicker one which had been made to look worse by being sprayed a nail-varnish pink. I threw my hat on the bed and painfully stretched out my legs.

Like a nerve-exposed tooth which yet must be violently seized, my father's death governed all my thoughts. Why was I a parricide? My father's illness had shown to me how deep my affection ran under the casual and chaffing relationship which had existed between us when we had lived alone after the war. I had always respected his wishes, and with no sense of strain. Even when I had poisoned him his pain had distressed me to the point of unbalance.

I bent down and loosened my shoe laces. Then I got up and lay on the bed. I was shatteringly tired. I tried to burrow through the distress and confusion in my mind to the clear simple past. Was there a time, far distant, when I hated my father? Against all reason, but in correspondence with my deep unease, it seemed to me that there was; that the murder which the events of my childhood had tried to force on me was *his* murder. Hatred could be buried for years beneath the easy commerce of family life – forever, unless the agent insanely throws off the sanctions which the family and society impose upon his primitive desires.

The rim of the light bulb, protruding below the pink-fringed shade, hurt my eyes. I closed them against it. The inhaler of coal gas, before the carbon monoxide kills him, is made to vomit by the other, less-deadly components. The face turns cherry red. I thrust my hand into the aperture of my waistcoat and felt my heart beating, my chest warm under the shirt. I tried to realize that it was I who was lying on the bed in the London House Hotel; Harry Sinton, who had been born, grown through childhood into an organism of complicated thoughts, and must die, finish, be as though he had never existed. . . .

Five

I

I opened my eyes and saw the curtains framed by a grey vagueness. It was morning, then. I was not surprised to find myself alive. Just as when I got up and drew the curtains and found that the street was wider, quite other, than I had thought it the night before, so my situation seemed changed, offering other possibilities than my suicide. I was stiff and cold, my mouth parched, my chin rough with beard. I could smell the smoke from my cigarette – a curious and alien odour. A postal van passed, a cat came up the area steps of the house opposite, but the street still had a fundamental emptiness and quiet.

I put a shilling in the gasmeter and lit the fire – a situation as ironically comic as a poem by Hardy. But I knew that I should not kill myself now that it was light. I felt my daytime qualities of toughness and ability – my father's qualities – rising again, moving me out of myself against the objective world.

Suppose it was fantasy that I had poisoned my father. Or even suppose that I kept the possibility of my unnatural act to myself: could I bear it? Would it fade harmlessly into the past like a *faux pas* or the loss of a valuable? I stared at the flames that roared up the hollow bones of the fire. No one knew that father's death was other than natural – not even Rimmer, for I had left him before the mood of abject confession had made me blab my guilt. And my killing had been wished, had come out of my true self. If I had to live I must resign myself to an altered, permanently sad existence, like a man who has suffered disfigurement or amputation.

Crouching in that unsavoury room, at that unearthly hour, scruffy, alone, my thoughts furious, I was very far from sane. It was almost an hour before I forgot my father and remembered that I was being hunted for the murder of Max Callis.

2

Somehow the time got to eight o'clock and I was able to go down for breakfast. The dining-room proved to be in the basement. It was distempered bile green and dominated by a huge Victorian mahogany sideboard on which little else stood but bottles of sauce. On the tables, at each place, was a bowl containing a few cornflakes. At one table sat a clerkly figure who said good morning. I took a seat: there was a jug with just enough milk to dampen the cereal which had probably been put out the night before for it resisted the teeth like thin cardboard.

'You'll have to ring for your tea,' said the clerk. 'The bell's on the sideboard.'

I got up and tinkled and a maid eventually appeared, Irish and with a lot of hair. With the tea she brought a plate of baked beans on toast, like an old squeezing of raw sienna on a palette. I ate some toast and marmalade and drank a lot of tea. The clerkly figure went out with another good morning: off, no doubt, to his desk at the Prudential. It was appalling to think of him living here, knowing how to obtain tea, that Thursday was baked beans morning. I lit a cigarette. I had all the time in the world, for it was no use phoning Charles Legge before the middle of the morning. In this basement I was as safe as anywhere in London.

The maid reappeared to do some clearing away: she, too, had a cigarette going. 'Didn't you want y'r bhaked beans?' she asked.

I said I didn't. She sang a few bars of a song of the day, and then said: 'Will you be in to dinner tonight?'

I said I wouldn't, that I was leaving after breakfast, going back to Lancashire. 'That's a great pity,' she said, in a complimentary way, and went out with the dishes. No one else came in for breakfast and when at last I went upstairs the hall was deserted. I got my hat and coat, and left.

Now the streets were full of people going to work, and I mingled with them, walking towards Bloomsbury. It was astonishing to think that only a mile away was my flat, the centre of the hue and cry. In Russell Square I bought a newspaper at the newsagent's on the corner and went into the barber's shop of one of the great red brick hotels. While the man cut my hair I looked minutely through the paper: there was nothing either about Callis or about me. For some reason the police were keeping their investigation quiet. Or could it possibly be that Fay had not, after all, spoken to the police – that her telephone call was for some private help? I sat, watching the scissors making me more and more presentable and commonplace, with a new access of cunning and zest for life. So would sit, I thought, those psychopath delinquents whose moral sense is entirely lacking. I put the newspaper down and the man tilted me back to shave me. The saloon was warm and its perfumes seemed luxurious: I could easily go to sleep, even after my six hours of sleep. The soft hand rubbed the lather on my chin.

'The hallmark of the psychopath is homosexuality' – the phrase, recalled suddenly from some book I had read, took on a fresh and personal meaning. It was as though Clarence Rimmer's probing of my emotions in the Corydon had unsealed all the involuntary adhesions in my brain, releasing discovery after discovery about myself. I remembered at school, in my sixteenth year, a master called Kevill who taught my set English Literature – an enlightened man who had shown me that poetry meant not 'A thing of beauty is a joy for ever' but 'In my veins there is a wish, And a memory of fish'. I comprehended clearly how I had always thwarted Kevill's personal approaches to me, keeping our relationship on the basis of others' follies, not our own. Kevill must have been homosexual, and now, as I saw the lather brush poised above me again, I regretted with all my heart that I had not surrendered to his affection and protection, had missed the initiation into true feeling that he might have given me, as he had initiated me into proper intellectual pleasure. It did not disgust me that that surrender might have involved acts in which I had never participated and which were contrary to my whole orientation.

I remembered, too, the day dreams which had haunted me in late months – the imaginary voyages with the adolescent crew. And my great love for my father; what was that but abnormality? My hidden hatred for him, too. Everything bore out my guilt.

The razor started its gentle scraping and the barber said: 'Nasty raw day, sir.' I recollected that I had heard that same phrase yesterday, in the midst of my wanderings, my convulsive effort to prove my innocence. The therapeutic effects of my wonderful night's sleep were finally dissipated: the old gnawing came back to my solar plexus; the delusions once more started to stand round me. If only I had the courage to snatch the bright blade which hovered over my face, and the certainty it would be my own throat I would draw it across!

3

Charles Legge was about forty, not fat but with a roundish face,
the skin of which looked loose and unhealthy. His bald head was
fringed with wisps of ginger hair, like theatrical crêpe hair, and
true to form he was wearing a thick lovat tweed suit and a bow
tie with green spots. In the thirties he had been a rather dim poet:
he was still dim but the times had become more auspicious for
his particular lack of talent, and in certain circles he had a reputation as a dramatist. In his plays, which were written in verse,
the characters usually started off in modern situations but soon
disclosed themselves as Biblical figures acting out their original
roles with alleged contemporary significance.

On the telephone I had arranged with his secretary to meet
him at the inquiry desk at Bush House. When he came along I
suggested a drink and we adjourned to Short's Wine Bar. As we
went he said: 'I've just been recording Morgan Foster – a perfect
script and a perfect delivery.'

'You do yourselves well on the Near Eastern Service.'

'It's surprising,' he said, complacently, 'what can be accomplished with a little care on a limited budget. That's something
they'll never learn at B.H.'

'Ah,' I said.

We went through the swing doors into the barrelled gloom of
the bar. 'Now, what will you have?' he asked.

'No, no,' I said. 'This is on me. Your expenses don't run to
drinks at eleven thirty, I know. What is it to be?'

'I'll have a glass of Marsala,' he said, admirably in character.

We took our drinks to one of the tables.

'I was sorry to miss your brother on the telephone yesterday,'
he said.

I skated quickly over the join. 'We want to do something
about Max Callis – and naturally you were the first person we
thought of.'

He nodded his inadequate red wig and said very seriously: 'I
see.'

'We haven't found out who his literary executor is –'

'Knowing Max,' Legge interjected, 'I shall be very surprised if he made a will.'

'And we don't know,' I continued, 'what he left in the way of manuscripts. There will be some uncollected poems, naturally. What we are toying with is the idea of a short memoir which could either come out as a pamphlet or the introduction to Callis's literary remains, as it were.'

He swallowed it all at one gulp. 'I see,' he said again. I observed that he had a habit of portentously nodding. 'I'm honoured, of course. But for Max's sake I shall be very glad to do it. His death is a tremendous loss.'

'You knew him pretty well, didn't you?' I fished.

'Yes,' he said. 'Though only since the war – since just before I published *The New Romantic Revival.*' This was his frightful collection of essays on modern poetry. 'Perhaps you know the book?' he added.

'Yes, indeed,' I said.

'I wasn't content just to delineate my subjects through their poetry. I made it my business to see them all, to talk with them, to find out how they lived, what they thought about all sorts of things not directly connected with literature. It was a new idea and didn't prove too difficult – except in one or two instances. Callis was one. He was in this country towards the end of the war but he went abroad again in 1946 and was still abroad while I was writing my book. I wrote to him through his publishers, his old publishers – your firm hadn't started then, I think – but I got no reply. I discovered later that he never answered letters. I made some inquiries and found that he was living in Sicily. So the year before last I used my holidays to go to Taormina to see him.'

'Most enterprising.'

'It's a rather strange story,' said Legge, with relish. 'He was ensconced in a broken-down house absolutely penniless, with a Maltese girl who had left her husband for him. The girl had brought her three young children as well – I don't think any of them belonged to Max – and he looked after them while she worked as a waitress in a restaurant. What a ménage it was! Max was writing nothing, just getting more bloated and more indolent. He wanted to get away but simply hadn't the means. He'd gone out with an advance from his publishers to write a book on the islands of the Western Mediterranean and hadn't done a stroke towards it, and now the advance was exhausted. Goodness knows what would have happened to him if I hadn't arrived at that particular time. The authorities were beginning to regard him with great suspicion – not only because he was so down and out but also because he was dabbling a bit in a tobacco racket to get money for drink. He drank, you know.'

'So I've heard.'

'Well,' said Legge, 'to cut a long story short, I brought Max back to England.'

'Not with the Maltese.'

'Of course not. I expect the girl went back to her husband: though she was rather a slut she was a hard worker and I daresay she'd be quite welcome.'

'What did Callis do when he got over here?'

'He always left his personal relationships in a mess,' said Legge. 'I think when he was in the States during the war he actually got married, but he never spoke about his wife. I must say I liked Callis, in spite of himself. He aroused the Christian virtues in one. And I admired him enormously as a writer. I pride myself that if I hadn't intervened in Sicily there would have been no *Microbe in Command* – a much underestimated book, as I'm sure you'll agree since your firm published it. He was living in my place while he wrote most of that – an astonishing poetic burst. And he did a series of talks for me – those and a few other odd jobs kept him in beer and cigarettes. I'm sure if he'd gone on staying with me this frightful tragedy wouldn't have happened.'

Charles Legge sipped the last of his Marsala. 'Will you have another drink?' he asked.

'Yes,' I said, 'but let me get them – I asked you out.'

'Nonsense,' he said, feebly.

'I insist,' I said and went up to the counter. Callis's death was like the last episode of a serial which the reader who has missed the other parts must try to interpret on the flimsiest and most baffling evidence. How had Callis got into the quite expensive block of flats which Rimmer also inhabited? How long had he been taken up with Fay? How had he spent his last hours? And how had I caught up with him, engineered our solitary interview, and killed him? Once again, bearing in one hand the gin and in the other the Marsala, I had the frightening sense of frittering time away while my adversaries, purposeful, knowledgeable, drew tight the net. I must ruthlessly suck Legge dry, and quickly.

But he was a hard man to hurry: he was the sort that in his life has sat hour after hour before a glass in the corner of the *Wheatsheaf* or the *Fitzroy* or his local, satisfied to pour out his complacent ideas on art and life before anyone uncritical or drunk enough to sit with him. He had, I remembered, an earnest wife of repellant aspect to whom he talked at parties when no one else was available and who answered him seriously and at length. I took the drinks back to our table.

'So Callis left your house,' I said.

'Yes,' said Legge. 'Your good health, Sinton. We've got another protégé living with us now – a young artist called Gerald Wilkinson. He's still a student but he's going to be good. I feel that now both the aristocracy and the bourgeoisie have decayed it's up to artists themselves to patronize their younger brethren. Don't you? After all, most of us have a spare room and a little more spaghetti in the pan in the evening doesn't ruin us.'

'You lost touch with Callis after he left you?' I prompted despairingly.

'He went to live in a flat in Sickert House. Don't know how he managed to get hold of it or pay the rent. That was about a year ago. I used to see him sometimes: he was never properly sober. I shall always remember meeting him one afternoon going up the steps of the Tate – it was the opening of the Polynesian Art exhibition. He said: "I've just been lunching with my benefactor and a very special lunch it was. A bottle of brandy on the table afterwards – that shows how much he loves the art of poetry." He looked terrible, and all his buttons were undone except those done up on the wrong hole. I put him to rights before we went in. There was a speech by Herbert Read or someone. Right from the start of it Max was muttering. Then he began walking round the gallery and saying out loud: "What a lot of fuss over a load of crap!" I got him out among the shushes and tut-tuts before the attendants could reach him, and took him downstairs to the lavatories.

"Crap," he said. "Polynesian crap." Then he was sick. But vomiting never seemed to affect him much. I led him into the restaurant and bought him coffee and he talked the whole time. "All art is crap," he said. "I've given it up entirely in favour of leisure. It's the duty of those who know how to live to get supported by those who know how to make money. Not waste their lives producing crap. I always thought that work was evil – even crap-making. Now I know." I told him not to be such an idiot, not to waste his talent. But he was very far gone. About a month after that I saw him talking to two shady characters under the Warning Low Archway – boys with crew cuts and jackets down to their knees. I didn't stop.'

'When was that?' I had somehow to pin him down to dates and facts.

'Oh, this winter,' said Legge. 'In a way I blame myself for not being more interfering. When I saw the way he was going I should have tried to get him back home. Perhaps I shouldn't have succeeded but the effort would have salved my conscience. But one doesn't see things that afterwards seem inevitable. I was inexpressibly sorry, of course, when I read of his death, but I wasn't surprised. No, not really surprised. You see he tried to kill himself while he was living with us.'

'He tried to kill himself?'

'My wife came back from her posture class one afternoon and found Max in his bed, under the clothes, with the gasfire turned on. He was drunk and the gas hadn't affected him at all, but I'm sure it was a serious attempt.'

I could not work out the implications of the irony of this. I saw clearly all the details of my room at the London House Hotel, and felt my face grow scarlet as though Legge had discovered some intimate and disgraceful secret that concerned me. Indeed, I was so sure that he would suspect my too-violent reaction that I once more took the glasses and returned to the bar counter.

'Really, Sinton,' said Legge when I came back with the drinks, 'you should have let me buy these, you are making me feel most guilty.'

'Think nothing of it,' I said.

'Your good health,' he said. 'I must come here more often. This Marsala is quite excellent.'

I dared to put the question. 'You think it was suicide, then?'

'Well, of course,' said Legge. 'What else could it be? Murder?' He laughed – in a curious snorting way as though he were blowing his nose without a handkerchief. Then his face straightened. 'Oh, I see,' he said. 'Misadventure. No, the poor chap killed himself, I'm sure. Perhaps something to do with that tarty Fay Lavington he was going about with – do you know her? I've wondered whether I ought not to telephone the police and tell them of the gassing attempt, but I've come to the conclusion that it would do no good – certainly not to Max's memory. It would have to come out at the inquest and the papers would get hold of it. And I haven't been round to Sickert House – didn't want to intrude on the relatives and so on. I expect the police have found them. There was a brother in I.C.I. and a sister who lectured at the London School of Economics – barbarians, Max called them and never had anything to do with them. I suppose they didn't want to have anything to do with him, either.'

'How did he die?'

'Shot himself,' said Legge.

'At – at Sickert House?'

'No. Didn't you see it in your newspaper? In those embankment gardens by Cheyne Walk. Awful to think of him walking in there alone – sitting on a seat or going into the shrubbery.'

I tried to remember how I had enticed Callis into that place but there was roaring in my head that prevented thought. I drank my gin, lit a cigarette, looked round the bar, hoping Legge would go on talking, fearful of his questions, longing to leave him but in a ferment to squeeze the last drop of information out of him – like a soldier making a reconnaissance of enemy ground.

Legge said: 'The strange thing is – it's haunted me ever since I heard about his death – the strange thing is that I saw Max on Monday night. I believe it was the first time since I'd seen him with those Soho figures. And, of course, now I think of it I see that he simply looked at the far end – an awful colour, a frightfully puffy face. I should have made the effort and gone to him. Only he was in the stalls and I was – er, upstairs. And then after the show was over I lost sight of him. You see even then he must have been contemplating it.'

'Where was this?'

'At the Haymarket,' said Legge. 'This adaptation of *The Possessed*. Have you seen it? It's really not bad at all. Quite an impossible task actually to cut the thing down for the stage, but it certainly revives one's feelings about the book. Even makes parts of it more vivid. The man who plays Shatov, for instance, has a great shock of almost-white blond hair – a little thing but it seems to make all that part real: I suppose because one fills in the background with one's knowledge of the book. Dostoevsky's very greatest, don't you agree?'

'Was Callis alone at the theatre?'

'No,' said Legge. 'He had this Fay girl with him. Good-looking girl. Max had something, you know, for women.'

My jealousy blazed up and made me almost inarticulate. 'Do you think so?' I said, astonished at the malice in my voice. 'That face, those filthy clothes, that sullenness.'

Legge looked a little alarmed. 'I can see *you* didn't care for him. Still, I must admit Max rather hid his good qualities under a formidable bushel.'

If I could feel like this about the man dead, what furies must have filled me while he lived, while he filched and violated my dearest possession! My character of killer was as distinctive as a uniform: it baffled me that the police had not long ago taken me as I wandered about in my half-hearted undercover.

I said: 'No one saw the – the act?'

'The shooting? I don't know.'

'There've been no broadcasts and so on asking for eyewitnesses to – what's the phrase? – come forward?'

'Not so far as I know,' said Legge. 'Now about this memoir. I'd like to get it clear in my mind before we part – and I'm lunching with Stephen at 1.15.'

'The memoir?' For a moment I could not think what he was talking about.

'What about length? If it has to stand on its own I suppose it ought to be about ten thousand.'

'Yes,' I said.

'And I expect you will want it pretty quickly.' Legge looked serious. 'I've promised to write a little play for the centenary of

St Paul's, Greenwich and there's not much time. But I expect I could deliver the memoir by the end of May.'

'That would be fine.'

'And payment? I suppose we ought to be horribly mercenary and discuss that.' Legge snorted down his nose again, and we fixed up terms. He said: 'Will you tell your brother how grateful I am to him for giving me the opportunity of writing about Max? He's a great man, isn't he? Always got his finger on the pulse of things. Goodness knows what modern literature would do without him.'

4

I came out of Short's, crossed the Strand and walked towards Charing Cross, past the jewellers having their thousandth closing-down sales, the shops selling surplus American officers' clothing, the Woolworths, the Saxone, the Halifax Building Society. Hat-less clerks, and executives with black homburgs, moved towards their lunches; male or female students, wearing scarves down to their thighs, made for King's College; a few provincial parents pulled their children in the direction of Trafalgar Square. I had to work things out, I told myself, put my facts in order, extend the plan that so far had preserved me. The sandwich bars were crowded to the doors, taxis edged past with their flags down. At one of the entrances to the courtyard of the station two police-men were standing, with apparently nothing to do but scan the passers-by for the faces of thieves and murderers. My fear leapt in my belly and I dodged into the courtyard so that I should not pass in front of them, and then threaded myself through the parked cars, and came out at the other entrance. I turned left, by the open shop that sells toffee apples, ice-cream and souvenirs. The people were comfortingly thick.

I went into the Corner House, through the foyer and the purchasers of chicken patties, bath buns, soused herrings, and up in the lift to the self-service. Shuffling along in the queue I tried to reconstruct the end of Callis's life. After the theatre he goes with Fay – to the Corydon perhaps. He sleeps – not at her

flat, for I could believe her statement that there was nothing in
their relationship; I must believe it, in spite of her lie when she
said she hadn't seen Callis for days – he sleeps almost certainly at
Sickert House. He gets up the next morning to the last day of his
life. The murder must take place after dusk. Remembering my
experience with Charles Legge I could see how easy it must have
been for me to call on Callis and entice him out, as far as the quiet
embankment gardens. The revolver was his, obtained by him for
suicidal purpose from his frightful Soho contacts.

A girl in front of me said to her friend: 'Shan't have that mince
again, will you?'

Her friend said: 'Naow. What you going to have?'

'Liver sausage salad, if it's on.'

'Are you really? Can't stand liver sausage.'

The queue crawled forward. Could it be possible that I had
shot Callis at such close range that it appeared that he had killed
himself? And wiped my prints from the gun and escaped from
the gardens unseen? The police had only to enquire of Legge or
his wife to discover Callis's suicidal tendencies. I saw all at once
the tragedy of life that arranged its facts so conveniently for the
establishment of my innocence, but left my conscience with so
unbearable, so inescapable a load of guilt. It was the same with
my father's murder. And – the old memory stabbed my heart
with its cowardly sudden blow – it had been precisely the same
with the death of John Fraser.

Now I had reached the food counter. A moving belt, with
which one had to keep pace, carried a tray remorselessly past
the ranged viands, forcing one to adjust unnaturally one's appe-
tite with racing time. My hand hovered schizophrenically over
the meringues, the dishes of rice pudding, the rolls, the salads,
the fried fish, the welsh rarebits, the lamb stew. At the end of
it I found myself paying for a heterogeneous collection I knew
I should never eat. I found a vacant seat at a table occupied by
some grave, newspaper-reading men. A fat woman with an eton-
crop was playing a tune on the electric organ which took me back
to my last night's ordeal at the Corydon. Slowly I unrolled my
cutlery out of the paper napkin in which it was wrapped.

Rimmer had said that there was something else, something

as cataclysmic as my father's death which my consciousness had buried but which had added its hidden force to the depth of my breakdown. Of course, he had been right: my life was all of a piece. As I cut my food and chewed and tried to swallow it I lived through that other day of horror eight years ago.

I had known Fraser right from my entry into the Navy. We had done all our courses together, were much of an age. I hated him from the moment I came across him – hated him physically and for his character. He was big, very pale, with golden hair that rose from his forehead in tight, narrow waves. His personal habits were careless and untidy – at our training establishment I was class leader, and it was he I was always up against in my tussles to get discipline, he who let the mess down at inspections and drill. But he wasn't unintelligent or incompetent – it was just that he took things with that degree less seriousness than was required of him. He worried me; perhaps I even feared him. I would rather have done his duties for him than have to remonstrate with him when he failed with them.

That period passed, and on our technical courses I was surprised at the ability he displayed. I found myself secretly trying to better his performances in our tests, with the rather ridiculous rivalry of one schoolboy and another. In the smaller classes we were thrown closer, though I never remember that we went out together. In spite of myself I could recognize the ability which our training drew out of him, until I realized that lackadaisical and bloody-minded though he had been at the start he was going to be an enormously competent officer. Our first appointments separated us and in the ensuing nine months I forgot all about him.

Then, early in 1942, I went to a squadron at Port Reitz in East Africa. Fraser was already there. In the most extraordinary way I found that my former dislike of him had vanished: we greeted each other as though we were old friends, our past experiences together formed a basis for a couple of evenings' drinking and after that we were inseparable. I found his mind sharp and intelligent about our situation, our companions, the service. We quickly created a private mythology of jokes against our superiors, the food, the climate, the aircraft we had to fly in, our slightly absurd present role in the war.

Our afternoons were usually free. Some of us would drive a truck out of the oppressive clearing in the palm trees which was the airfield and along the coast to a gently curving bay. In peacetime this had evidently been a recognized bathing place: there was a large but ruined reed hut and, about fifty yards from the shore, a concrete pillar projecting from the water. At the side of the pillar an iron ladder enabled one to climb to the top and dive. The sand of the bay was nearly white, moving with innumerable crabs: the water almost too warm for swimming.

One afternoon the truck, for some reason, was not available. Fraser and I decided to walk out to the bay – his passion for swimming was as great as mine and we had the stretch of blue water to ourselves. We swam far out, and came leisurely back and fooled about in the shallows. Then we smoked, lying on the sand, observing the strange habits of the crustaceans, until once again we were unbearably hot. We swam to the concrete pillar.

It all happened quickly and, like so many tragedies, had strong elements of the ludicrous and avoidable. When we were both on top of the pillar and the water round it had settled down we had a clear view of what on our previous visits had always been obscured by the antics of other swimmers – the astonishing shoals of fish that flashed round and nuzzled against the concrete, their stripes, their spots, their diaphanous fins, visible through the limpid water. Below the water the base of the pillar was rather eroded: the fish were able to disappear into its cavities, among the trailing weeds. Fraser got off his stomach and said: 'I'm going down for a closer look.' And he dived perpendicularly to the pillar. After half a minute he came up. 'Wonderful,' he gasped. 'There are some anemone things lower down. If the water wasn't so buoyant I could stay down longer. Perhaps I could hold on to the ladder.' He swam round to the ladder side and dived from the surface. I was really observing all this with no more attention than one gives to anyone's private activities when bathing, so that it took me a few moments to realize that Fraser had been under water too long. In the next moment I thought that he was pulling my leg and that he had swum round the pillar below the surface, but of course when I looked he wasn't there. Even then I stood and scanned the water all round the pillar before I dived down by the ladder.

The sea was so clear I could see at once what had happened. Either accidentally or, what was more likely, deliberately, so as to keep himself down, Fraser had hooked his toes in a rung of the ladder that lay below the surface. The rungs here were all bright green with weed: at some stage the pressure forcing his body to the top had wedged his foot further between the rung and the concrete, so that he was held fast by the whole ankle, his already unconscious body fluttered by the tide, as a held bird flutters.

Before I could touch him I had to come to the surface for a breath. Then I went down again. The space between ladder and pillar through which his foot must be pushed was much narrower than I had imagined. I got hold of his foot but against the weight of his body it would not turn to the proper angle for release. I twisted the foot, panic-stricken: it was like a puzzle in which two interlocked shapes can only be drawn apart by a certain precise gesture of the wrists and fingers. I was forced to surface before I had achieved anything.

I glimpsed the sun and sky through smarting, throbbing eyes, and then dived again. This time I pushed the ankle brutally, but with no effect. Little coiling threads of blood came from the abrasions. Below, I could see Fraser's gently moving hair and clouds of small striped fish. I came hopelessly to the surface, gasping in the air, and once more forced myself down to him.

In the end I had to hold on hard to the ladder to recover myself, coughing the water out of my lungs, fighting down the sickness. I scanned the arc of the bay, the palms thrown oddly, like darts, into the blanched sand. There was no one in sight, and Fraser still rocked to and fro below, caught in his trap. Quite soon there was nothing for it but to make the cruel swim to the shore. At every stroke I felt I was betraying and deserting him, and a half a dozen times I nearly turned back, only my intelligence telling me that it would be unavailing. Reaching the shore I pulled on my shorts and shirt and began running towards the town. Twice I met groups of natives and hovered, sweating, a moment before them, imprisoned helplessly in my barrier of language. Hot air quivered above the road, the sun flamed on my bare head. At last I stopped a car driven by a European and he took me to get help.

At the inquiry I was commended for the efforts I had made

to save Fraser, and I had much public and private sympathy for what was called the ordeal I had been through. But the stupidity of his death haunted me for months, years; and all that time contained deep fissures of misery in which I imagined that it would have been easy for me to have dived again, to have moved more skilfully that trapped, pathetic leg, to have rescued a being more courageous and accomplished than myself. At such moments I remembered with agony my first loathing of him, and saw my later friendship as a sly veneer to conceal a deadly antagonism that had cunningly waited its opportunity to wreak malice.

I pushed away my lunch and pulled the coffee towards me. The memory – more vivid, it seemed, than the long-past event, had set me trembling, brought a choking lump to my throat. The wedding-cake ceiling was oppressively low, the noise of the electric organ like some nerve-wracking distraction from an abstruse mental process. The coffee would not go down, and it seemed as though my companions at the table were watching me gagging at it. I reached under the chair for my hat and hurried out between the tables through the clinking of a hundred knives and forks and the hum of talk that persisted like the noise of some operation of manufacturing, my white image following me along the mirrors set in the imitation marble of the walls.

At that moment I was almost at the end of my tether. The progress I seemed to have made since I left my flat in understanding my situation was wholly cancelled. The building, the people struggling in and out of it, gave me a suffocating claustrophobic sense, and I felt the old violent, desperate anger rising in me again. The facts surrounding the deaths of my father and Callis had become inextricably tangled with my imaginings about them. I said to myself, almost audibly, as I clattered down the staircase: 'You're ill. You shouldn't have to bear this. You're excusably, dangerously, ill.' And confronted by the maze of traffic in Trafalgar Square, the whirring of pigeons and the spray from the fountains, I looked round for one insane moment for a policeman, to whom I might surrender the unbearable load of the future.

Without any conscious purpose I wandered past the National Gallery, past Hampton's, and round into Haymarket. In a few seconds I found myself among the vermilion and cream pillars of the theatre, gazing automatically at the displayed photographs and at a board which said: MATINÉE TODAY – and knew that as in a game where the victim is led to a pre-decided object by the mental concentration of the other players my motion had been directed to a place which had contributed its mite towards my fate. The women of the suburbs, the visitors from the provinces, the holders of complimentary tickets, those with mid-week half-days, were already moving up the steps into the foyer. I followed them without question, and at the box office secured, with a dreamer's mastery of his material, a single ticket in the stalls.

5

The play began almost as soon as I took my seat, but its words passed over me as though they had been in the Russian of the novel from which it had been adapted. I could think of nothing but that night in this place less than a week ago, when Callis, alive and unscrupulous, had sat next to Fay, brushing her elbow, leaning to speak to her and feeling her hair against his cheek, watching at will the fetishes of his desire – the small ear nipped by its ornament, the start of the moulding of her breast, the slight curve of thigh under the dress. In the darkness I pressed my thumb nails into my forefingers as though I were undergoing a physical pain.

Gradually my surroundings forced themselves into my consciousness. I suppose I had read *The Possessed* during the craze I had had for Russian novels in my teens but I had forgotten all details of its plot and characters. When my taste developed I found I could not share the modern admiration for Dostoevsky: though I saw many of his virtues I could not stomach what I considered his artificial and self-conscious contempt for materialism, the things the war had taught me to value – democratic organizations, atheism, liberty and all the rest. I had never re-read *The Possessed*.

On the stage, with a background of a seedy room, two young men were enacting a scene to which I listened with a growing unease. One of them was pale and dark, with the simple, child-like manner of the typical Dostoevsky hero. The other, more ordinary, was taking the role of the interrogator. This was their dialogue:

THE DARK MAN: I'm just trying to find out the reasons why men daren't kill themselves. That's all.

THE INTERROGATOR: What do you mean 'daren't kill themselves'? Are there so few suicides, then?

THE DARK MAN: Very few.

THE INTERROGATOR: Do you really think so? [*The other rose from his hard kitchen chair and began pacing to and fro.*] What stops people from committing suicide?

THE DARK MAN [*Halting and gazing at the other*]:Two things. Only two – one very little, the other very big.

THE INTERROGATOR: What's the little thing?

THE DARK MAN: Pain.

THE INTERROGATOR: Pain! Do you really think that at such a moment pain can be of any importance?

THE DARK MAN: Certainly. Of the greatest importance. You see there are two kinds of suicides. Those who do it emotionally – because of great sorrow, or from spite, or because they are mad. They do it suddenly. They don't think about the pain: they just do it suddenly. But some suicides do it through reason – and *they* think a great deal.

THE INTERROGATOR: Do you mean to say that there are people who kill themselves through reason?

THE DARK MAN: A lot. And if it weren't for superstition there would be more – many more. Everybody.

THE INTERROGATOR: What, everybody? [*The other continued his pacing.*] But aren't there ways of killing oneself painlessly?

THE DARK MAN [*Stopping in front of the other once again*]: Imagine a stone as big as a house. It is suspended and you are under it. It falls on you, on your head. Would it hurt you?

THE INTERROGATOR: It would be frightful.

THE DARK MAN: I'm not talking about fear. Would it hurt?

THE INTERROGATOR: A stone as big as a house? No, I suppose it wouldn't hurt.

THE DARK MAN: But while you are standing there under it you would certainly think it would hurt. The most profound philosopher, the most skilful doctor – they would think it would hurt. Everyone would know that it wouldn't hurt, and yet everyone would be afraid that it would hurt.

THE INTERROGATOR: And what about the second thing that prevents suicide – the big thing.

THE DARK MAN: The next world.

THE INTERROGATOR: Do you mean punishment?

THE DARK MAN: Punishment's not important – just the next world, the other world.

THE INTERROGATOR: What about atheists? [*The Dark Man did not answer.*] You're judging this from your own experience, aren't you?

THE DARK MAN: Everyone must judge from his own experience. There will only be absolute freedom when it's just the same to live or not to live. That must be the aim for everyone.

THE INTERROGATOR: The aim? But perhaps when it's achieved no one will want to live.

THE DARK MAN: Of course. No one.

THE INTERROGATOR: But surely man fears death only because he loves life. That's how nature's arranged it.

THE DARK MAN: That's where the lie comes in. Life is painful and terrible and man is unhappy. But man is not yet what he will be. There will be a new, happy man for whom it will be the same to live or not live. Everyone who wants absolute freedom must dare to kill himself. And he who dares to kill himself has found out the secret of the lie. He is God. But no one has done it yet.

THE INTERROGATOR: But there have been millions of suicides.

THE DARK MAN: But not for the right object. Not to kill fear. . . .

At the end of the first act I wandered out of the auditorium, past the ushers bringing trays of tea for the ladies of the audience, full once more of the thoughts of self-destruction that had haunted me for the last weeks and that I imagined had reached their climax at the moment last night when I had quitted the Corydon. I returned to the image of the switch. I adumbrated, as I had so often, that there was a switch above my head, within reach of my hand. I had only to press it to cease to exist. Would I go through the simple action? Before, I had really known that I could never make that tiny pressure. It was true, I had loved life too much, even in my morbid and neurotic state. Life was painful and terrible but nature had arranged things so that man could bear the pain and terror, even use them for the ends of his character.

But now, as I walked through the foyer and into the street where coming out of the dark theatre the afternoon sun seemed untimely and cruel, my self faltered, cringed, before the ordeals it saw before it. Life was disgusting, as food was to the mortally ill. In that instant I believed I could have stretched out and pressed the switch. And I knew, too, that what had dissuaded me in the hotel last night was not the fear of pain: I could regard almost with equanimity the stone suspended above me. Last night some of my love for life remained – the lingering and occasional affection that just prevents a husband from deserting his ageing and long-married wife. My continued existence depended on that fragile and discontinuous thread.

The bell rang and I went like an automaton back to my seat. And now, notwithstanding the agitated distraction in my mind, I began to follow the story that the play unfolded, as in spite of oneself one reads in a dentist's waiting room. There even seemed something meaningful for me particularly in this drama of the cynical, evil man, the young Verhovensky, whose cold-blooded, almost uninterested actions precipitate a series of the most frightful cataclysms in his little community. The scene especially between him and Kirillov – the simple Dark Man of the first act – where he is trying to persuade Kirillov to write a confession to the murder of Shatov which young Verhovensky has planned came over with the cryptic significance of a row of cards for a fortune teller's victim. Since Kirillov intends to commit suicide, it cannot matter to him that he is to confess to a murder of which he is innocent, but he makes difficulties. Both men have revolvers. During the argument Verhovensky draws his out. And then Kirillov suddenly snatches his from the window sill where it has been lying throughout the scene.

VERHOVENSKY: Oh, oh, so that's it is it? [*He aims his revolver at Kirillov.*]

KIRILLOV [*Laughing angrily*]: You brought your revolver, didn't you, because you thought I might shoot you? But I shan't shoot you ... though ... though.... [*And in his turn he aims his revolver at Verhovensky. But slowly his hand drops and finally, gasping and trembling, he puts his revolver down on the table.*]

VERHOVENSKY [*Who had kept his revolver levelled intently until the last moment*]: All right, you've had your little game, and now it's over. I knew it was only a game, but you ran a risk, I can tell you. I might have fired.

KIRILLOV [*Pacing up and down*]: I won't put down that I killed Shatov.

But in the end he writes the confession; and later comes the extraordinary moment of the suicide. The stage set had been arranged so that one wall of the room ran diagonally. In this wall was a door leading to a further room. Kirillov suddenly seizes his revolver and runs through the door. Verhovensky reads the confession through, lights a cigarette, listens at the door, walks to the table again, says aloud: 'If he begins thinking, he'll never do it.' Then he takes up one of the candles lighting the room, goes to the door, and cautiously opens it. From the darkness Kirillov rushes at him with a terrible roar. Verhovensky slams the door shut and leans against it with all his weight. The sounds behind it die away and once more there is a deathly quiet.

Verhovensky walks about, lights another cigarette, stubs it out, draws his own gun, and again goes to the door with the candle. Awkwardly, his hands full, he turns the knob. The door creaks: he jerks it open with his foot and takes a few steps into the little room, holding the candle high. The room seems empty. 'Kirillov,' he calls, 'Kirillov.' Verhovensky walks to the far end of the room, looks about in a puzzled way, and examines the window. Then he turns and in the light of his candle sees – as the audience with a gasp suddenly sees – in the niche made by a cupboard and the wall, Kirillov standing motionless. His arms are held stiffly by his side, his head is thrown far back as though he is trying to hide himself. Verhovensky, after a moment of paralysed horror, rushes towards this figure, shouting and stamping with his feet. Kirillov does not move. Verhovensky holds the candle close to the face, so that its pallor and fixity are illuminated. And then it can be seen that Kirillov bends his head and bites the hand holding the candle. The candle falls and is extinguished: the sole lighting on the stage is the single candle in the main room. Dimly Verhovensky can be seen raining blows with his revolver on Kirillov's head: then stumbling over chairs, the table, he rushes into the main room. Kirillov shouts after him in a terrifyingly loud voice: 'Soon, soon, soon, soon, soon!' Before Verhovensky has time to get out of the main room there is a shattering explosion, and the body of Kirillov falls heavily half through the door.

For me the illusion of this scene was complete: it did not seem to be played by actors on a stage. I sat rigid, the skin of my skull suffering formication as at some violent and emotional passage for full orchestra. The events of the drama seemed to be changing my whole attitude to life: I could no longer predict with certainty what my actions would be when the play was over and it was my own existence which had to be experienced.

6

A little dazed by the light, the chattering groups, the taxis drawing up to the theatre, I stood on the pavement of the Haymarket, struggling into my overcoat. I moved off in the direction where the emerging people offered the least resistance. Nevertheless I bumped into a man coming out of the Gallery exit.

'Hello, Harry,' said this man, and I saw that it was Robert Midwinter.

'Hello, Bob,' I said, thinking how I could get away from him quickly.

'Been to the play?' he asked.

I said I had. We were on the terms of Christian names, but I had never been really intimate with him. We had in the first year of the firm published his quite remarkable study of Poe, written not from the obvious psychoanalytical but the no less rewarding sociological angle. He was a man of about forty-five, of proletarian origins, with the knobbly face of a pugilist and sparse hair so closely cropped that his head looked as though it had been made from grey soap.

He said: 'You can see why the thing's such a success in spite of all its seriousness, et cetera. Anything anti-Russian, anti-democratic, can be made anti-Soviet without the least alteration. Chronology doesn't matter: all these people place it post-Revolution or don't bother to place it at all. The atmosphere since 1944 has been compounded to just the right fogginess for everything to be dim and therefore effective in the sphere of ideological pressures!' He always spoke very rapidly, his ideas rising so thickly in his mind that he never had time to develop them with any lucidity, or even give his speech grammatical coherence. He was coatless and hatless: in the breast pocket of his jacket was a battery of fountain pens, as though he used them all simultaneously, as he wrote, to accommodate the flood of ideas; under his arm was a formidable collection of books and periodicals.

'That scene of the meeting,' he went on. 'The comic dialogue and the irrelevant theoretical discussion of the so-called revolutionaries, which takes place in reality, of course, but which isn't the true essence of such meetings. And all the ideas – "socialism spreads principally through sentimentalism" et cetera.'

It looked as though we should never move: the crowds filtered away, the taxis stopped crawling down Haymarket, dusk was falling. 'Come and have a pint,' he said at last.

'Will they be open?' I asked, feebly.

'Just,' he said, and stumped off purposefully. It seemed to me that he was wearing the same navy blue trousers, the same tweed jacket that he had worn at those cultural receptions in Kensington Palace Gardens where I used sometimes to meet him in the honeymoon days with the Soviet Union at the end of the war.

We went in a pub in one of the little streets between Haymarket and Lower Regent Street. 'This universal craze of the West for Dostoevsky – succeeding the healthy craze for Tolstoy of the war years – shows the hold that mystical ideas have taken, everyone finding an apology for turning back to Christianity, for their disillusion with political action, et cetera. London' – Midwinter moved his glass in comprehensive circular direction

– 'a decaying mass of reactionary ideas, hopelessness, unfaith in human potentialities. Everyone turned in on himself.'

'Dostoevsky's as fashionable an intellectual occupation as cricket,' I said and then relapsed into my stupor, wanting to go and with no place to go to. My life had become as rootless as a tramp's, a series of undesired encounters; and these days had been singled out by some magnifying power of time that made them all monstrous detail; the dreamlike insight of a slow-motion film. The bar was still quiet: the barman read the evening paper and an old man fed a packet of biscuits to his correspond-ingly old fox terrier.

'You won't mind me being blunt,' said Midwinter. 'Take your firm's list – how it's changed over the last three years. All the old dead-beat idealists coming back again, the covers and typography of your books getting more and more ornate and the contents more and more art for art's sake, further from ordinary life, how it's lived by the majority. And that magazine your brother edits – what's it called? *Pavilion* – it's only *The Yellow Book* and bile.'

I saw his point and tried to take an interest. 'I think you're a little unfair to Laurence. After all, he's not truly creative himself – he can only make his bricks with the straw that exists.'

Midwinter gestured with a hand that somehow had contrived to be as coarse as though he made roads instead of writing with it, and launched himself off on three simultaneous themes, like the passage in the *Mastersingers* Prelude. And then, perhaps his solid presence acting on me like a disbeliever at a séance, the sedi-ment in my mind suddenly precipitated itself.

All at once, as when one's usual chair is occupied and one sits and sees a long-familiar room from a new and curiously strange aspect, I saw the possibility that my father's death had been natural. I saw myself like Laurence, of the same normal blood, our easy mastery of the world springing from the same civilized circumstances, sharing a grief enormous but not excessive. Like Midwinter, I could visualize guilt and anguish over-laid unneces-sarily on simple human facts and emotions.

Midwinter talked on, but now I paid no attention. With grow-ing excitement I grasped the logic of what followed from my innocence of parricide: I need not have killed Callis. As one for years misreads a line of familiar verse, I saw the other pattern made by the facts about Callis that Rimmer and Legge had given me. The increasing indolence, the increasing prosperity: somehow, from someone, Callis had been extracting money – money in quantities sufficient for a flat at Sickert House, beer in the Corydon, stalls at the Haymarket. The plot was blackmail, not jealousy.

I looked at Bob Midwinter, at the brewers' advertisements on the dark panelling of the bar, at the lean familiar hand round my glass: this was not illusion. In the dark tunnel I could see the disc of light I had left long ago – and also, it seemed in that moment, a similar glimmer ahead of clarity, of freedom from fear. What I had to do was to map this blank episode of my journey; map it with instruments of intelligence and courage, do deliberately what I had blindly, instinctively been trying to do ever since I had escaped from imprisonment yesterday morning.

'One point,' Midwinter was saying, 'about Orwell's 1984 is the extreme shoddiness – the domestic servant's novelette shoddiness – of the love passages. If that's his vision of that side of human affairs, what reliance can be placed on his political vision, et cetera?'

I nodded. Some day, I promised myself, I would deepen my acquaintance with Midwinter. His boxer's face, the too-small grey jacket, the collar and tie awkwardly put together, coalesced in a touching sincerity: and his stream of ideas ran transparently over a sterling sincerity, an absence of guile.

'I once gave my little daughter *Animal Farm* to read,' he said. 'Afterwards I asked her: now who do you think the villain was? Do you know what she said? The farmer. You see, Harry? Not Napoleon, or even Snowball. And, of course, that *should* have been the point of the book. But Orwell had no love for the working class.'

I nodded again. Someday – but now I must get away.

7

Of course, it was too late for the office – as I realized as soon as, in the call box by the safety deposit, I had dialled the number. I heard the telephone ringing and imagined the little suite of rooms in Southampton Street that blue-grey paint and furnishings from Storey's had made presentable, even elegant. It seemed to me then so clear that the record of our dealings with Callis, or Laurence's or Miss Hind's knowledge of him, would provide the clue, the link I wanted, that Rimmer and Legge had been unwilling to supply, that my disappointment and sense of time slipping wasted by aroused an acute panic. Quite recklessly and irrationally I came out into Lower Regent Street and hailed a taxi. 'Where to, guv'nor?' asked the man, as I already had the door open. The answer came pat off my tongue, though my mind was in confusion. '7 Esher Square. I'll show you the house.'

The taxi turned left at the lights, past the queue forming at the Plaza, and down Jermyn Street. Laurence might be at home, I reasoned: even Miss Hind, who often before dinner went there to work on *Pavilion* or Laurence's extra-publishing activities. I kept thinking that if the guilt about the deaths of my father and Callis were a guilt mainly of the mind, as I had felt over Fraser, I could bear it. It was the worldly attributes of punishment that I really feared – arrest, trial, the noose, my physical extinction. Through the windows of the taxi came the coloured lights, the purposeful couples, the warm breaths of basement gratings, the bright interiors glimpsed through swing doors, of the West End at night – in which I was hopelessly involved. The creative existence, the realm of ideas, Kirillov's all-sufficient brain – these were utterly alien, beyond my powers. I had strayed into them like a slave into the wrong room of a palace.

And yet, as the taxi drove down Knightsbridge, I began to feel a disquiet – a disquiet not entirely mine, as one goes to renew acquaintance with a companion whose last meeting has been at some shared disaster. There are embarrassments as painful as bereavements. I even ridiculously hoped that the taxi would be involved in an accident and I should be prevented from ever reaching Esher Square.

I marvelled that Laurence could have brought himself to live in that house, impregnated as it was not only with the sad events of father's death but also of our childhood. I realized, as I had so often realized before, how different we were. Of course, my father had specifically devised Number 7 to Laurence in his will: by taking up residence there Laurence was only devoutly carrying out father's presumed wish. But the will had been made several years ago, when my father no doubt envisaged that at his death Laurence would have a wife and family: it was really far too large a place for a bachelor.

My mother, too, had died in that house – in giving birth to me: Laurence must remember that as well. And with that thought came the realization that I bore the guilt of the death of both my parents. I leaned forward on the worn leather seat transfixed again by the vision of the terrible repetitive patterns my life had made.

The driver pulled aside a panel of the glass partition and put his ear to the gap. 'Which one, guv'nor?' he said. I looked and instantly orientated myself. 'The first past the lamp.' There were no watchers on the pavement: only, as I alighted, the cat Joe galloped across the road and down the area steps.

Six

I

I knew the precise shape of each worn step which led up to the porticoed entrance. I noticed that Laurence had had the front door painted an unfamiliar primrose. With only a moment's hesitation I pulled the bell. Instead of Baker a young maid opened the door: it must have been Baker's day off – surely Laurence could not have got rid of him.

'Is Mr Sinton in?' I said.

'No,' she said. 'He's not home yet. Can I take a message?'

'You're new, aren't you? I'm his brother. I'd like to wait for him.'

'Oh,' she said, her training not having taken her this far.

I could see the black and white tiles of the hall floor and the enormous ugly urn that held walking sticks and umbrellas. With a pang I distinguished the malacca cane that my father had used, that I remembered from my infancy accompanying our Sunday walks in Kensington Gardens. Through the door of the little garden room behind the dining-room the figure of Miss Hind emerged: she looked at the open front door, saw me, and came hurrying.

She dismissed the maid and took me back into the garden room. It was quite unfamiliar: there were two walls of bookshelves and two desks, one with a typewriter; a plain amber carpet; many bowls of flowers. Laurence must have thought my father's study upstairs too big and cold.

'Is Laurence coming home for dinner, Hindy?' I asked.

Miss Hind was eyeing me with an expression. 'Are you all right, Mr Harry?'

I remembered that I hadn't seen her for two months. I said politely: 'Yes, I'm much better, thank you.' But her expression did not change, and I understood, with a stab of fright, that she had some knowledge of my flight.

'What's the matter, Hindy?' I said.

'Mrs Giddy telephoned the office today,' she said.

'I see,' I said. 'Of course.' Even at that moment it occurred to me to wonder why Thelma Hind was so concerned about me. After all, I was only one of her employers: she could easily get another job and walk right out of my life. For the first time in all our acquaintance I looked at her as a woman rather than as a piece of business apparatus. Perhaps she was still not yet forty: perhaps inside that tall heavy body, cruelly decorated with rimless spectacles and more than a suspicion of a moustache, fluttered the soul of a young ardent girl. She tried very hard – at her work, at understanding the nuances of the literary world, at her dress. She followed the changes in fashion with a religious fervour – appearing sometimes in little felt top hats or hats like cartwheels, pinched-in waists and short flared jackets, military shoulders and long jackets – but to no avail: she could never achieve grace. She tried too hard. I said: 'Mrs Giddy fusses. But I suppose I should have let her know that I wouldn't be back today.'

'She said one of your friends was ill.'

'That was a story for her benefit,' I said. 'She has become a tyrant. I've got to find excuses to stay out the night, just as though I were married.'

I walked to the window and looked into the little paved garden at the tree into which it was possible to escape with a book, and the revolving summer-house that on fine evenings in the old days used to be redolent with the smoke of my father's cigar.

In a few moments, when Miss Hind could see that I was quite normal, I would begin to ask her about Callis.

I heard her come up behind me. 'Mr Harry, please don't think me interfering. But I wish you'd tell me what the trouble is.'

'What trouble?'

'You do think I'm interfering,' she said. 'I'm sorry. But after all I did work for you, and – ' She was incoherent with a quick rush of emotion. 'You haven't been in the office since January.'

'Oh, that,' I said.

'Mr Laurence said a nervous breakdown. But it has always seemed so strange to me that *you*. . . .'

'Yes, I've had a nervous breakdown.'

She ignored my reply. 'Was it anything to do with the office? A quarrel?'

'A quarrel with my brother?' I smiled, and could have laughed outright.

'Well, yes,' she said.

When I thought about it the conception of my falling out with Laurence did not really seem absurd. I had a sudden memory of our youth, of my seizing a stick almost as big as myself from that frightful piece of ceramics in the hall and rushing murderously at him. I said: 'No, of course I haven't quarrelled with Laurence.' I found my legs aching and sank down on the window seat. 'Have a chair, Hindy, and don't look so serious.' She sat at one of the desks, behind the typewriter. 'Did you say that Laurence *was* in for dinner?'

'Yes, he'll be in soon. He simply has to do some work this evening.'

Why on earth should I have hated Laurence so furiously in that long-distant past? Was I a monster, whose education and family had coated with a thin crust of civilized behaviour, now cracking, disintegrating? I saw Miss Hind looking at me over the typewriter, and I could not discover the feeling behind her look, though it filled me with foreboding. I said, half jokingly, half with irritation: 'What's the matter, Hindy? Have I got a smut on my nose?'

'Oh, Mr Harry,' she said, still ambiguous.

I said rapidly: 'Look, Hindy. I think you can help me. I want some dope on one of our authors.'

I don't think she heard me. I saw her hands go to her face and her head drop below the typewriter, and I got up in alarm. 'What is it?' I said. 'What is it, Hindy?'

Her shoulders were shaking slightly: for a moment I thought she might be laughing. Then she raised her head, her glasses askew, her mouth open, lipstick smudged. 'I don't know,' she cried.

Then I divined what she was going to tell me. And despite all I had suffered it was as though for the first time I was experiencing the reality of my actions. And this reality consisted in the pale yellow walls, the books, the new carpet, the disarranged figure of Thelma Hind, becoming in a moment utterly phantasmal, and an intense dread rising from my stomach and breast and becoming the whole of my experience.

'The police came to the office this afternoon,' she said.

Nevertheless it was incumbent on me to continue living. I heard my voice like the thin voice discernible among the scratching and roaring of an ancient gramophone record: it even mimicked the expressions of a real voice. 'The police? What did the police come for?'

'Mr Laurence saw them. I wasn't in the room, of course.'

'Of course not, Hindy.' I was continually astonished at the miracle that permitted some part of me to go on participating in ordinary life, as though after some frightful mutilation I had been fixed up with an ingenious apparatus for speech, for holding a cigarette, moving my eyelids. 'But you found out afterwards what it was all about?'

'No,' she said. 'Not everything. Mr Laurence was terribly upset: he wouldn't – couldn't tell me everything.'

'What did he tell you?'

Her spectacles had become misted: she took them off and her

eyes regarded me with a fresh surprise and innocence. 'There must be some confusion,' she said fervently. 'Things must have gone wrong somewhere. You see, I know you. We've been together for so long. I can't help speaking to you like this; I can't help it.'

'What did Laurence tell you?'

'Mr Callis is dead. Shot.'

'Yes, Hindy?'

'They were inquiring about it. They wanted to see – you. They were looking for you. They'd been to your flat and couldn't find you. Then they came to the office.'

'What is my brother doing now?' I said.

'Why, he's looking for you. He was going to your flat, and – and other places where you might be.'

'What other places?'

She looked as guilty as though it were she who was the murderer. 'Miss Lavington's?' she said, tentatively.

I opened my mouth to speak again, but I felt the thing grip me – that apparatus of time and events – and carry me forward in its own way, to its own destination.

'What happened?' asked Miss Hind. 'What have you done?' But it seemed to me that she didn't want to know.

I tried to make my voice calm. 'Hindy, I must find out all about Max Callis. I've tried everywhere and now I've had to come here.'

'What have you to find out about him?'

'How he died. Why he died. And that means I must find out how he was living, what he did on that last day.'

She put on her spectacles and made a feeble attempt to push back the wisps of hair that had escaped from her bun. 'I don't understand what has happened,' she wailed. 'I don't understand a thing. If the police are looking for you about – *this* – why don't you know?'

I half meant to break down. 'Oh Hindy, I'm in a terrible mess.'

'Don't, Mr Harry. Please don't.' She came from behind the desk and hovered over me, like someone who would like to but dare not put an animal out of its misery. 'Mr Laurence will be back soon. He'll know what to do.' She offered me these words as though they were aspirins and tea.

I said: 'But if he brings the police with him – '

'Why should he?'

'It's dangerous for me to stay here. You knew Callis, Hindy. Tell me.'

'Well, he – ' She broke off and looked utterly perplexed. 'But what is there to tell? We published his poems, you know.'

'That was years ago, Hindy.' I felt the signalled time of departure remorselessly approaching, and myself achingly, uselessly, far from the scene.

'Not many years,' she said. 'Then there was his book on Constantinople.'

'We didn't publish that,' I said, my nerves on edge.

'Oh, no,' she said, 'of course not. It wasn't written.'

'How could it be a book, then?'

'He was going to write it,' she said. 'He was going to Constantinople. It was to be part travel and part history. We commissioned it and he had an advance. If you don't remember, Mr Harry, it must have been after you were ill.'

'How much?'

'I beg your pardon?'

'How much advance did he get?'

'I think it was £250.'

'Not bad.'

'Well,' she said, 'there were his travelling expenses.'

'But he never went to Constantinople, did he?'

'No,' she said, 'but of course, he was going. As a matter of fact, Mr Harry, I think there was another advance after the first one. A smaller one.'

But even this could not be all Callis's sudden prosperity. I said: 'He got a second advance before he'd started off?'

'Well, there was the historical part. I think he was doing the research for that.'

Callis was like a ghost: approached, one's fingers went through him. 'He must have come to the office about all this,' I said desperately.

'Oh, yes,' said Miss Hind. Her eyes avoided me. 'And here. As a matter of fact he came here the day before – the day before his death.'

The phantom loomed closer. 'Tell me about it.'

She raised her hands in a gesture. 'There's nothing to tell, Mr Harry. Naturally, I turned it over in my mind as soon as I read about him in the papers – before today . . . and the police. But there's nothing to tell.'

'What did he come about?'

'The book, I expect.'

'The famous one on Constantinople?'

'I was here working,' she said, 'and I spoke to him when he arrived, but of course I wasn't with him when he saw Mr Laurence.'

'What did he say? What did he look like?' It was like trying to drag some significant memory of a great dead personage out of a stupid old retainer.

'He looked as he always did.' I could see her trying. 'His hair was sticking up a bit, his shoe-laces undone. He might have been tipsy but I don't think he was.'

'Did he say anything?'

'Oh, Mr Harry. I can't remember.' She was near tears. 'I expect he said the usual things. Nothing that mattered. He never used to speak to me more than was necessary. Not that there was reason why he should. Mr Laurence will be able to tell you what passed at the interview.'

'Yes,' I said. But I did not know whether or not I should stay to see Laurence. It was not only that I suspected that he believed in my guilt and would at once betray me, but also that I feared him. He was the one person in the world who knew all my life and who could reproach me for what I had made of it. I saw in that moment how like my father he was – not physically, but in his stern regard for truth and integral conduct. This search of mine for an alibi Laurence would condemn not because it was futile but because he believed that one should take the consequences of one's actions, face up to punishment. It must have been my mother who had transmitted to me the evasive, cowardly, too-sensitive veins of my character.

It was in this room, at the time still in its character of a breakfast room – and used by my father and me for all meals in the winter – that after my father's death Laurence and I had discussed our domestic plans. Now that the house was his, now that all its associations were painful, I had wanted to leave, but I don't think I should have taken the actual step if Laurence had not made plain the issues, even secured for me the lease of the place in Luxor Street, and arranged for Giddy to accompany me. Already at that time I was beginning to imagine the terrors that in the solitariness of Luxor Street had become dense and real. Once I must have been capable and decisive, but my father's death had been the signal for me to lapse into an almost feminine state of remoteness from affairs – to lapse so completely that I could scarcely imagine myself existing in the world of contracts, cheques, money.

2

Out of the corner of my eye I could see Miss Hind watching me as I prowled slowly between the window and Laurence's desk. We had nothing more to say to each other, though I knew that, for her, unspeakable questions formulated themselves behind the barrier made by the conventionality of our relation which even yet had not been broken down. On the white wall the second hand of an electric clock scanned the dial at an enormous pace. I did not know what I was waiting for.

There was a little stack of page proofs on Laurence's desk. I picked one up and opened it. What did I expect to find – a miraculous manifestation of Callis's book on Constantinople? A paragraph of print stared up at me.

'The medical experts have tried to convince us that the prisoner is out of his mind, that, in fact he is a homicidal maniac. I submit that he is not out of his mind, that if he had been he would have behaved with more cleverness. As for his being a maniac, I would agree with that, but only in one sense: that is, his *idée fixe* about the three thousand roubles. But I think it is possible to find a much simpler motive than his unbalance. I myself would agree entirely with the young medical witness who maintained that the prisoner's mentality has always been normal, and that he has simply been irritable and exasperated. The reason for the pris-

oner's continual and violent temper was not merely the money:
there was a deeper motive for it. That motive was jealousy!'

For a moment I thought that the book had been specially
printed, to trap and torment me. My first impulse was to call out
to Miss Hind, to ask her what it meant. The next instant I decided
to behave as though the book were ordinary, innocent. I flicked
the pages over casually, back towards the title page.

'That's the new translation of *The Brothers Karamazov*,' said
Miss Hind, without prompting, 'that we're putting into the Chel-
sea Library series.' I thought that her tones were those one uses
to humour an imbecile.

'Very interesting,' I said. How could the time be found for this
kind of conversation? I came to the title page, which confirmed
her statement, and immediately my old memory of the novel
rose up, confused but vivid – a memory of a father at a window
and his son below armed with a brass pestle, of blood drying on
clothing and handkerchiefs, and a long interrogation and trial.
Suicide, parricide – these fantasies of Dostoevsky had come,
like a text in a chance-opened Bible, to show me the realities and
meaning of my life.

I said to Miss Hind: 'What on earth is my brother doing? Why
doesn't he come?'

'I am sure he won't be long,' she said placatingly.

Could I have harmed him, too? I turned to conceal my face
from Miss Hind, my toes flexing and unflexing in my agitation.
I tried to account for all the hours of my day: images of Charles
Legge, of the play, of Midwinter, rose up – images which seemed
insufficient to cover the great stretch of time. How easy it would
have been to meet Laurence, go up to him with a weapon in my
hand, and kill him! He knew about Callis, he could have easily
discovered the secret of my father's death: he had always been in
the utmost danger from me. Was that why I had agreed so readily
to leave this house?

Miss Hind said: 'I think he had gone to look for you.'

'I hope he never found me,' I said, and laughed.

'What do you mean, Mr Harry?' she said, nervously.

I shook my head. 'Nothing, nothing.' I sat down at Laurence's
desk: there was an enormous leather blotter and a silver table

lighter that I had never seen before. 'How is Laurence getting on, Hindy?' She looked puzzled. 'What's more important, how are you getting on with Laurence?'

To my surprise she started to weep; it was like a casual bang at a broken-down radio which suddenly gets the thing going. I said: 'Is he beastly to you?' She pulled off her spectacles – those non-concomitants of emotion – and wiped her eyes, but didn't reply. 'Loyal Hindy!' I said. 'You'd burn at the stake for the firm, wouldn't you?'

'It's my fault,' she said with many gulps, 'I get on his nerves and I don't always understand what he wants. I wish you would come back to the office, Mr Harry.'

It was the village speaking of its alien life to the visiting exile. 'I wish I could come back,' I said, but that wish was not mine: the possibility had passed beyond desire. I humoured her, who could still take the simple life seriously. 'You ought to leave, Hindy. There are plenty of jobs for an efficient slave like you.'

'I couldn't leave now.'

'Because of – what's happened to me?'

'No,' she said, 'not entirely – it's – '

And then I stopped listening to her. I heard my father's step in the hall, on the tiled floor: the sound I had heard all my life and which seemed to me to have roused only a sense of guilt, the frightening knowledge that the misdeeds of the day, which till then I had been able to suppress, even at times forget, must now be confessed and the punishment for them be suffered – a punishment not merely of conscious infliction but residing also, most, in the understanding that I had caused the punisher the pain of disappointment and anxiety. Involuntarily I moved quickly away from the desk, taking with me the Dostoevsky proofs which I examined unseeingly, with over-acted absorption, as though the discovery of me at this and not another occupation could somehow add to my virtue. Laurence came in at the door. I realized that I had known who it was all the time.

'Harry!' he cried, and I saw with surprise his face whiten, as though it was he who had dreaded the encounter. In a quieter voice he said: 'How long have you been here?'

Though in actuality it was only a few weeks, it seemed as

though a great epoch had passed since our last meeting, a surprise of time like that depicted in the last part of Proust's novel. Laurence looked to me taller, his shoulders huger, the prematurely bald front of his head round which the hair grew curly and black, more extensive, than I had remembered; and yet at the same time his appearance seemed to come from the remote past of our lives, from the childhood in which our relationship had been closer, our emotions towards each other fiercer, unclothed by convention and civilization. The clothes he was wearing – the soft serge navy blue suit, the white linen, the blue, white-flecked tie – were, like the room and the apparatus on his desk, unfamiliar but inevitable, incorporated immediately into the nexus of common memories which bound us.

'I had to see Hindy,' I said. I was preternaturally conscious of the proofs in my hands, thick but flexible.

Laurence turned sharply to Miss Hind, who had already risen and was shifting away uneasily. 'I'd like to speak to my brother alone,' he said. She went out without looking at me. Laurence came closer and fixed me with his ice-blue eyes. 'I've just been talking to Fay Lavington.'

I glanced beyond him involuntarily as though it was in this house that he had met her and that I could expect to see her following him into the room. And then I felt a pang that she was not here, and that someone had been with her without me.

Laurence said: 'She told me everything that happened between you yesterday afternoon.' He removed the proofs from my hands as though I had been a child and took hold of my arm and ushered me on to the window seat, sitting very close beside me. 'Harry, I'm terribly sorry,' he said simply.

It had never occurred to me that anyone could feel pity for me, or even that my condition was such as to be capable of drawing pity. The sudden realization of my plight in the eyes of those who might be sympathetic induced reciprocal pity in myself, and without any attempt at concealment – for at that moment I was quite incapable of exerting any further strength – I wept. Laurence's arm came round my shoulder and I heard from far off the murmur of his encouragement.

At last I was able to take a cigarette from the case he was holding out: I drew the smoke in with only the tiniest pleasure – the momentary interval while the dentist changes his implements.

'Fay told the police – you knew that?' he said. 'And when they couldn't find you the police came to see me. How did you manage to avoid them?'

'I've been trying to establish my alibi.'

The words must have come to him as indistinctly and mean-inglessly as they seemed to me, because he didn't appear to take them in. 'What made you do it, Harry?' he said, getting up and walking abstractedly to his desk. 'It's a nightmare, an absolute nightmare.' He turned and presented his large smooth face, the decisive nose, the long upper lip as calm and authoritative as some great prelate's. 'I can't help blaming myself, Harry. I should never have let you leave here after Christmas when I knew how upset you were about father's death. And I should have seen you more often during the last weeks. But I never imagined that you were as – as ill as you are, that you had this animus against poor Callis, or even that you were in love with Fay. You're such an independent fellow: you've never confided in me and you know I don't like to pry.'

'I'm sorry, Laurence,' I said.

'Oh, my dear boy,' he cried, 'I don't want you to be sorry for me. But when these terrible blows come down one can't help feeling guilty. I feel I didn't look after you well enough, when it was my duty to look after you.'

'You're not my keeper,' I muttered.

He came back and sat by me on the window seat: I smelt the faint odour of the after-shaving lotion he always used.

'Now what is there to be done?' he said, not questioningly but merely as he set his mind in order. And then in a different voice, he asked: 'Was there a fight, a struggle? Max could be very violent.'

'I don't know,' I said.

'What do you mean, Harry?'

'I don't remember.'

'Harry,' he said, 'we shall have to go to the lawyers. I'm think-ing of self defence and all that sort of thing.'

'I don't remember. I simply don't remember.'

'That's what Fay said you told her.' Laurence put his hand on my knee. 'But it can't be true, Harry. You must remember something of what happened – meeting him, going into those gardens.'

'No.'

His tones became almost wheedling. 'Don't be afraid of me. I want to help. There's no point in hiding the facts from me.'

'Do you think I'm mad, Laurie?' I started to ask the question almost detachedly, as though it were a debatable point which scarcely concerned me, but as soon as it was out I felt reality crumble and fall away from me, and I was left alone, in a position in which equilibrium could not be held, at the very moment when the cataclysm begins to operate on the involved human.

'Harry, Harry,' he said, but his troubled face contradicted his tones.

'It's only the mad who really can't remember their bad actions.'

'This is terrible,' he said, and for a moment leaned back his head and closed his eyes. 'I simply can't think – can't take it in.'

The isolated man has his terrors but also his compensations: he can be cunning and ruthless. I was free: after all this time I was still free and there was no reason why I should not continue to plunge twisting through the undergrowth while authority searched the outskirts of the wood. 'You saw Callis that day, Laurence,' I said.

'Yes, I saw him.'

'If you can place his movements you can place mine far away from them. That's what I meant – I've got to establish an alibi.'

'But how can you do that? The police will make their inquiries and nothing I could say would stand up to the truth. Your position would be worse than ever.'

I felt rage creeping through my arms and legs, like an invalid's returning strength. 'You won't help me?'

'Of course I'll help you, Harry. That's what I've been trying to do ever since I knew. I'll use every power. . . . But lying won't help.'

'You take it for granted that I killed Callis,' I burst out.

Laurence looked at me in amazement and I sensed his body

withdraw from me a tiny but horribly significant inch. 'I take it for granted?' he repeated. 'But you yourself told Fay – '

'Yes,' I said. 'I told her I killed him. But I'm not sure – I don't remember. My breakdown . . .' I tried to remember the clear terms in which Rimmer had almost convinced me of my innocence. 'My breakdown has revived all the feelings of guilt I've ever had in my life, Laurie. This isn't the only crime I've accused myself of. And that's why the alibi is so vital, Laurie. Don't you see?'

His face had become still more alarming to me. The man that I knew, that was my brother, that bore affection for me, had withdrawn to some remote location. 'But Harry,' he said, waiting patiently to get it in, 'Callis was shot with your revolver!'

3

The blood came to my cheeks and stayed there. 'How do you know?' The truculence was a thin skin over a morass of terror.

'The police told me. They traced it through the Navy.' Laurence made a gesture of despair. 'Why on earth didn't you hand it in when you were demobilized?'

I walked on trembling legs to the desk, to the bookshelves, to the fireplace. The whole of life had contracted to this room, this moment. 'I must go,' I said.

'What's that?' said Laurence. He got up and came to me. 'You see, Harry,' he said gently, 'if you can't remember, can't be sure, what happened – '

'You've got to let me go,' I said. I thought of the dark streets, the steps up to the London House Hotel, the cubicle at the end of the corridor with its seclusion and its gasfire.

'I can't stop you, Harry,' he said sadly. 'And I wouldn't if I could.'

'But as soon as I've gone you'll telephone the police.'

He turned away from me, pulling out the snowy handkerchief from his breast pocket, wiping his great forehead. I went on rapidly: 'And what about Hindy? We must get her back in here at once. She'll betray me for all her loyalty!'

'Not so loud, Harry,' he urged. 'Not so loud. This is intolerable. It simply can't go on!'

Yet it went on: the fire crumbled a little, the second hand swept round, the breath came and went through my mouth. And the bell rang.

'The front door,' I said.

'Yes,' he said, stalling.

'You've sent for them already.'

'Harry, how could I? You've been with me all the time. And why should it be them? It could be anyone.'

'You answer it,' I said.

He moved towards the door. 'Stay here,' he said.

'You mustn't tell them, Laurie. You've got to put them off. Promise me that.'

'I won't tell them,' he said.

But I didn't believe him: I went after him and grasped his sleeve. Then the door opened and the little maid appeared, and I took my hand away as though we were still boys and caught in some forbidden act. The maid seemed to understand nothing of the history of our attitude, which we now retained as though it were the last frame of a reel of film. 'Two gentlemen from the police, sir,' she said to Laurence without emotion.

It seemed miraculous to me that he could reply. 'Show them into the dining-room,' he said, and immediately I knew why he had said it. The dining-room was the first door away from the front door: they were being put conveniently away. I wanted to fawn on him: I tried to smile to show my understanding and gratitude, hoping he would turn and see the effort. The maid went out.

Laurence said: 'I'll go and see them. Follow me out in half a minute and go up to the drawing-room.'

'Yes,' I said. 'Yes.'

'I'll get rid of them. I expect it's only an excuse for a drink. I'll come upstairs when they've gone. We've got to get this thing straight, Harry.' He cast a glance back at me as though to fix me in his mind for ever. 'Stay in the drawing-room. I must know where you are. In case—'

'Yes, Laurie. All right. But go, go. They may come in here looking for you.'

He made his exit like one called away from an absorbing entertainment by an ambiguous message.

The real presence of fear is even worse than its anticipation. The sudden silence of the room seized me as though I were a forgotten man on a doomed ship. I went to the door too soon for safety, but the passage and the hall at the end of it were empty, and the door to the dining-room closed. I thought of my revolver, the hut in the barracks in Hamburg where it had been issued to me in 1945, the drawer of underclothing where I had kept it, the infantile – was it? – motive that had made me retain it. I walked quickly up the stairs, my hand on the poignantly familiar slenderness of the rail, the patterns of the iron banister all similar, yet each with its individual distinction of height and, as I knew, of aspect on the hall below.

The drawing-room was unchanged. There, with its back to me facing the fireplace, was my father's chair, high-backed, covered with greenish brocade. It was hard for me to believe that I should never see him in it again. It brought back to me the disturbing dreams I had had since his death, dreams of varying circumstances but with the same theme: my father was still alive and leading his normal life and I would be with him in this house or at one of the holiday places of our childhood. But I knew that he was mortally ill, and suffering as he had quietly suffered at Christmas, and I wished with all my soul that he were dead so that his pain would end. It could not be that pity was the only motive for these dreams: now I cringed with horror at their naked meaning.

I drew aside one of the curtains: below, against the pavement under the streetlamp, was a black car with a radio aerial. The blind, myriad tentacles groped for Callis's murderer. From my god-like isolation I suddenly saw the investigation at its slow, thorough, impartial work; listing Callis's friends and enemies, checking their opportunities, examining his papers, his laundry basket, the contents of his pockets. There was Clarence Rimmer, who lived in the same block of flats: was there any connexion between Rimmer's marital unhappiness and Max Callis? And Charles Legge, who had once taken Callis into the bosom of his family but of late had not been intimate with him. And Fay. I lived once again through the agitation she had betrayed when

I spoke of her in connexion with Callis's death: the investigation must above all include Fay.

I became so lost in my detective story day-dream, my futile list of suspects, that when I remembered the realities of the murder – the police below, the revolver, myself in hiding – a fresh wave of panic and astonished horror drenched my whole being, and I ran across the room and switched out the light. The drawing-room was an obvious trap: Laurence had sent me there, and I must do nothing suggested by others. Society's only interest in me was to lock me up. I stood just inside the door, out of range of the light on the stairs, and tried to imagine my future. But I could see nothing beyond this night.

My own old bedroom was on the next half landing: I went up to it almost automatically, as though it were still the time before my father's death. I remembered clearly my excitement as a child when I first moved in to it after being always with Laurence: the cupboards and wardrobe that were mine alone, the sense of large space over which I had absolute control.

I opened the door and my hand went to the familiar place of the switch. However, to my surprise the light was already on. All the furniture was the same as I had left it and in the old positions. But on the bed was a figure, not myself, who lowered the evening paper and said petulantly: 'Who are you?'

It was a youth who lay there on top of the ancient patchwork quilt (which through the years I had come to know like my face): he was fully dressed, except for his shoes, and on the bedside table was a bottle of hock and one of the tall green glasses. To find him seemed a logical extension of the nightmare, but the last twist that cannot be borne. 'Who the hell are you?' I asked.

'I say,' said the young man, 'you're awfully rude, aren't you. I'm staying here.' His voice was at once affected and proletarian: it was disconcerting to find a Newcastle accent having difficulty with its r's.

'With Laurence?' It was a question expecting the answer no: I could only imagine him to be a relation of the new housemaid, smuggled in illegally.

'Of course. I'm Adrian.'

'Adrian?' The nightmare was becoming farcical.

'Adrian Rossiter,' said the youth. 'I don't expect Laurence has told you about me.' He giggled. 'I'm on the run.'

I thought: this is my doppelganger, my distorted mirror-image. 'On the run what from?' I managed to ask.

'National Service, what do you think?' said Adrian Rossiter. 'You didn't think I'd done something wrong did you? The bastards wouldn't register me as a C.O. So I ran for it. Been a friend of Laurence's long?' There was a tone of anxiety and vague menace behind the casual question. I told him I was Laurence's brother.

'Are you really?' said Adrian, doubtingly. 'You aren't much like him, are you?'

I said: 'How long have you had my bedroom?'

'Ever since I came here,' he said. 'Is this yours then? You haven't been home for a long time, have you? Are you really Laurie's brother?'

I thought of the tall, immaculate, impressive man downstairs, and tried to connect him with Adrian's 'Laurie.' 'Yes,' I said, 'I'm his brother. Are you a writer?'

'Am I a whatter?'

'A writer,' I repeated. 'A poet.'

Adrian giggled again. 'Stop pulling my leg.'

'How did you get to know my brother, then?'

'Isn't he inquisitive?' said Adrian. 'I'm a friend of his. Can't I be a friend of his?'

'Yes, I suppose you can,' I said.

'Laurie's been very kind to me. It's not so easy when you're on the run. Laurie understands my troubles. He'd never give me away, you know.' Adrian gazed at me with a false trusting look, like a dog that has just done its mess on the carpet. 'Come and sit down, and have a drink. You can use my glass. That is, if you don't mind it.' The assumption was that I wouldn't mind it.

I went and sat on the ottoman at the foot of the bed: from this closer view Adrian was less pretty than I had thought. His flaxen hair started rather too low and went back at rather too acute an angle; the short nose was thickish; and there were shadows of decay between his front teeth. All the same I stared at him with fascination – the irrelevant clue that must be found in the end to have significance.

'Don't you want a drink, then?' he said. 'You don't come very near, do you? D'you know, I don't think you like me.' He turned off his elbow on to his back, and added, in the direction of the ceiling: 'My guess is you're not Laurie's brother at all. You're just jealous.'

'How long have you known my brother?' I thought: had Laurence even at Christmas a preoccupation like mine with Fay? And I remembered – and with the memory came the profound shifting and resettlement of the deep strata of my knowledge – Laurence's insistence, years ago, that he have a home of his own, though this house could have held the life that in my innocence I imagined him leading without it scarcely impinging on the exist-ence of my father and myself. One is curious about, one sums up and places the acquaintance; but those to whom one is closest are taken for granted, remain for ever un-understood, and therefore are capable throughout their lives of astounding one with their actions.

Adrian propped his back against the wall and smoothed his hair. 'Of course I'm only kidding you,' he said more amiably. 'I'm sure you're Laurie's brother. You look too nice to tell fibs.'

'You don't answer my question.' It was clear that he didn't know about Callis and me.

'What was it?' he asked, and then chattered on without wait-ing for a reply. 'It's nice to have someone to talk to. I get a bit bored, you know. It's not Laurie's fault, don't think that, but I have to be careful. I'm only going out at nights while the heat's on, and even then I never go in the boozers. You ought to come with us sometime, that is if Laurie wouldn't mind.' He tipped the bottle. 'Sure you won't have a snifter? Well, I've told you the story of my life – what about yours? What do they call you?'

I got slowly to my feet and went towards the door.

'Hey!' called Adrian Rossiter. I looked back at him: the dis-tance had once more composed his features into regularity and, as he leaned forward, his long hair falling over one ear completed, with the dark brows and glittering eyes, the illusion of a female impersonator. 'This is all in confidence, of course. I've treated you like a friend. I don't want what I've said to go no further. I don't know that I trust you now I come to think of it.' He put his glass on the table and made to get up. 'Has Laurie come in yet?'

'No,' I said, wanting to get away, appalled, bewildered. 'No, not yet. And don't worry: I don't like the police any more than you do.'

Adrian swung his stockinged feet back on to the quilt. 'Are you on the run too?' he asked.

4

We stood by the fire: it seemed that the occasion for sitting down would never come again. On the white mantelpiece the hands of the clock, under its glass bell, said four minutes to eight.

'They have no idea where you are,' said Laurence. 'They simply asked the same questions. They're very stupid.'

And they had gone: I had seen, on my return to the drawing-room, the black car curve away round the square, and felt the pressure lighten, the air become a little easier to breathe. Laurence smoked his cigarette as though it were some drug which had to be deliberately but urgently administered. At every turn of the conversation I thought of the youth upstairs: an embarrassment that cried out to be indicated but could never be, like the undone intimate buttons of a superior.

'Harry.' Laurence came so close that I could see the dark hairs that grew from his nostrils. 'What has really been happening to you during these three months? You've changed completely.'

His last words frightened me: yes, it was true, I had become another person. I could only give a schoolboy's answer. 'I don't know.'

'I couldn't have believed that this would happen to you.' Laurence, too, was moved. 'You were always so extrovert. You coped with school, the Navy. The last person.'

'Laurie, what do you mean by "this" – "this" happening to me?'

'Oh my God, Harry, you make it terribly difficult for me. You see I never thought when – when the police told me that you had shot Max – that I should see you again like this, like you are.' He managed to get it out. 'I mean normal, almost normal.'

'Yes,' I said. What he was saying was absorbingly interesting since it was about myself, and yet the picture it conjured up was of a stranger.

'You see, you understand so much, Harry. Apart from your memory of it, I believe you understand the whole thing. That's what makes it a thousand times more painful.'

I said harshly: 'Did you think I should come out from hiding a gibbering lunatic?'

His light eyes flashed at me. 'Yes. Yes, if you must know, I did. And I hoped for it. How can you bear what's going to happen if you're sane? My poor Harry, how can you possibly face it?'

I walked blindly to the table littered with magazines and daf-fodils. 'I can't face it.' I swallowed the choking regurgitation of self-pity and fear. 'That's why for these awful two days I've been trying to—' But the mass would not go down my throat.

'I don't know how to say this.' Laurence's deep tones pursued me. 'I don't know if it will be of any comfort. It's outrageous to have to utter it. But they won't hang you, Harry.' His voice quickened. 'I would never have told you what I'm going to tell you now. There was never any need to distress you with it. It was something that I could let haunt me alone.'

I went back to him. His words recalled the relations of our childhood when we had confessed easily to each other our hidden life, the relations that had been laid over with our later existence when though we met every day our deeper feelings were our own and we exchanged no more than acquaintances exchange.

He said: 'For three years after I was born mother was in a mental hospital.'

It was as though I had learned my true name after trying to get through life with one obviously false and inappropriate. 'How do you know?' I was astonished at the discrepancy between the casualness of the question and my emotion.

'Giddy blabbed to me ages ago. That's when she came to us, when I was born. I think as soon as she told me she realized what a frightful thing she'd done. She made me swear not to tell father that I knew: of course, I never could have told him, but she didn't understand that.'

I said: 'But how did I come to exist?'

'Mother came home, she was said to be cured. Giddy wouldn't go on with the details. All she said was that it was a mercy mother died at your birth.'

I wanted no details: they could be imagined, in their truth and clarity. And I remembered Giddy's fear of me.

'With this history – which Giddy could give – they must find you . . . not responsible.' I saw that what I had at first thought irregularities of the skin on Laurence's forehead were tiny beads of sweat.

'And then,' I said, 'and then they'll shut me up.'

'Yes,' said Laurence. 'Yes.'

I had thought that all that had happened to me had been accidental, contrary to my real nature: now I knew that the reverse was true, as I should have realized it must have been. No, I was not responsible, but with that knowledge there was no lightening of the load of guilt. The innocence and sangfroid of the insane exist only in the assumptions of the sane. I thought of the mother I had never known but had often tried, with curiosity and affection, to reconstruct, and found time to pity her for a confusion and anxiety that must have been even greater than my own.

'Father should have told me,' I said. 'How could he let me go through life not knowing what I was?'

'Yes,' said Laurence vehemently. 'He should have told you. It was unforgivable. That façade of normality he always maintained in front of his life – and behind it the sordid secret. And Giddy always there to remind him of it. But perhaps it wasn't a façade, perhaps the normality had grown solid all through. Father never had any imagination.'

I thought how curiously the qualities of our parents combine in us, so that sometimes what we thought we had inherited from the one proves, as we come to understand ourselves and them, to stem from the other. Laurence went abruptly with our glasses to the tray and poured some more scotch. He drank his at once but I could not swallow mine.

'What are you going to do?' he said, almost roughly.

I stared back at him hopelessly as I felt the dark amorphous shape of my crime and its retribution fill the future. In dreams one awakes and remembers that one's victim is really alive, but in actuality there can be no reversal: the terrible things happen and cannot be cancelled or averted.

Laurence turned aside and fiddled with the sword of one of the two little bronze Chinese warriors that stood on the mantelpiece. 'I haven't been sleeping very well lately,' he said. 'In fact, I went to old Riddell and got some tablets. Some barbiturate concoction. But I didn't use them after all – found I'd a prejudice against the things. So they're still in the little drawer in my bedside chest.'

Since he had ceased to speak of my fear I only half listened to him. It was not until he moved his position and fixed me with his eyes that I understood what he had been saying. Then he saw that I had understood. He said: 'Harry,' and then: 'What else can I do to help you?'

'Nothing,' I said.

'It's a good way out. No pain.' His eyes never left mine.

It was preposterous that we could talk like this of death, my death. Death could not be at once so melodramatic and so casual. At the approach of death the furniture should not continue to sit quietly about, gears change in the square, the clock hands point to an hour when the uneaten dinner would be spoiling in the kitchen. I went in imagination through the ordinary routine of going up to Laurence's room; finding the tablets and glass of water; quickly, without thinking, as though it were merely their unpleasant taste that was the barrier to taking them, cramming the whole dozen – twenty – into my mouth, gagging over them and feeling the hammer start its crescendo in my skull. . . .

'You mustn't be afraid,' he said.

But it was not fear that had kept me alive, that was still rooting me to this harmless room: the switch that can bring death was never actually under one's hand – always there was a margin of living which must be traversed before it could be reached.

'I'm not afraid,' I said.

Laurence managed a smile. 'No, I can believe that.'

'What about you, Laurie – the police?'

'You mustn't think about me.'

'Do you know, Laurie,' I said, 'I can tell you this now – before you came in tonight I thought I might have killed you.'

'Why did you think that?' I saw him steal a glance at the door.

'I don't know,' I said wearily. 'Because you weren't here and I couldn't account for you.' I thought that if my life could miraculously contain more time I might in truth kill him, as I had killed my father. I wondered if he knew that I was a parricide and a poisoner, and then remembered that no one shared my secret.

'Life is terrible,' Laurence said, wiping his brow with the immaculate handkerchief. 'Some would welcome the excuse to die. And the means.'

I took my glass of whisky and at last sank into a chair, feeling the blood move again in my legs. I heard myself sigh deeply.

Laurence moved from the fire. 'I'm going down to the study,' he said, and I thought for a moment that he was going to shake my hand or stroke my hair. He hesitated and then went on: 'I'm using father's old room now.'

'Of course,' I said.

He looked down at me from his world of utterly trivial and alien cares and desires, stuffing the handkerchief carefully back into his breast pocket. He opened his mouth as if to say something more, then closed it, and walked abruptly out of my field of vision. I did not turn my head, but I listened to his footfalls die away into utter silence. On one arm of the chair my left hand held the glass: on the other my free hand lay relaxed like a detached living thing whose heart was the little pulse that beat between the knuckles of forefinger and thumb. I watched the left hand raise the glass and pour amber fluid in the body that also appeared detached, as though, like some Wellsian creature, I had become all mind.

5

It was not intent that made me at length get up, but a sense of blankness, as one who waits for a distant train leaves his seat in the waiting-room and goes to pace the platform. And it seemed that I was watching myself cross the hall and walk slowly up the stairs; and both spectator and actor were quite without emotion. Perhaps this anaesthesia would last until the end: perhaps this

was all it was, the outrageous act of suicide, a few numb automatic gestures before the violent moments which could be suffered because they were irreversible. The body that normally was
myself had become the detached and almost ridiculous image
that I sometimes saw for a fleeting second in mirrors, whose fate
was a matter of complete unconcern.

I heard someone coming up the stairs behind me and at first did
not trouble to turn my head. Then Miss Hind's voice called my
name softly and breathlessly. I stopped on the landing and leaned
against the massive linen chest, waiting for her to catch me up. A
wave of weariness that was almost nausea flickered over me.

'What's the matter, Hindy?' I said, as she stood with one hand
on the stair-rail, the other holding her ample chest.

'Mr Harry,' she said. It was like bearing an interruption of
one's reading of an absorbing fiction. 'Where are you going?'

'To sleep.'

'Oh,' she said, and as she recovered her breath her air of
urgency dissipated a little. She looked rather embarrassed. 'Is it
all right?' she asked.

'Why haven't you gone home, Hindy?' I waited patiently,
scarcely irritated at all, for this irrelevant episode to end.

'I saw the police go away,' she said. 'I wondered if everything
was all right.'

'Yes, Hindy, everything is settled.' In the clarity of my exhaustion I saw the reason for the habitual turning aside of her head
I had always noticed when she spoke: she was embarrassed by
her rudimentary mandarin's moustache. Poor Hindy! Behind the
glasses and moustache, inside the unwieldy body, was the simple
wish to be beautiful.

'It can't be,' she said, 'can it?' Only the light from below, shining up through the apertures of the banister, illuminated us: it
seemed strange for her to be up here, where I had been frightened as a child by the dark and as a man by my father's pain. She
said, uneasily: 'Don't think I was eavesdropping, Mr Harry, but of
course I couldn't help finding out something of what was going
on when the police came to the office.'

'Of course,' I said. Soon she must go away and allow me to
finish the journey.

'And I can't understand it,' she cried, but not loudly, as though someone were concealed in the linen chest who must not hear her.

'Can't understand what?'

'Why they should want to ask you about the revolver,' she burst out. 'Were there two?'

'Hindy, I don't know what you're talking about.'

'You left your revolver here when you moved to Luxor Street,' she said.

Then I came back to the house to get it before I followed Callis. 'How could I have left it here?' said my voice.

'It was in a drawer of the desk less than a fortnight ago. I saw it when I was looking for some poems we'd lost that had been sent in for *Pavilion*.'

'What desk?'

'In the study.'

'Laurie's?'

'Yes,' she said, and this time she turned her full face and looked at me with eyes troubled behind the lenses. 'Unless there were two. But there couldn't be two, could there?'

'Did you tell him you'd seen it?'

'No, I haven't told anyone. Only you.'

There was a rodent gnawing urgently in my bowels. 'Why have you told me?'

She started to speak and then stopped, sketching a gesture. 'You see, it isn't in the desk now,' she said at last.

Suddenly the thing had gone far beyond my comprehension, the simple metaphor had been succeeded by the mathematical theorem, and the riddle once more rose remote and unscalable. 'Where's my brother now?' I said, though I had intended to say something else.

But she was busy with her own thoughts. 'When you weren't at your flat,' she said, 'and then when you came tonight – so different – ill . . . I thought it was your breakdown. I've been so confused. But I keep asking myself why there should be any mystery, why the police shouldn't simply be told the truth. Of course I can see that *you* couldn't tell them if you'd forgotten that you didn't take the revolver when you moved.'

'But Hindy, for God's sake what do they want to know?'

She averted her head: I could hardly hear her unbelievable words. 'Well, they know – it's all accepted – that Mr Callis shot himself – '

'They *know*?' I felt under my hand a strip of carving on the linen chest, so vividly that I could visualize precisely the little cherub face in its halo of rose petals.

'But they've got to clear up what Miss Lavington told them now they've found the revolver was yours, Mr Harry.' Her voice became emphatic, almost indignant. 'Anything you said to Miss Lavington was understandable if you'd had a nervous breakdown.'

'They know Callis shot himself?'

'Yes,' she said, as though it were unimportant. 'I gathered that. It was taken for granted. Naturally, they never say anything straight out. But, Mr Harry, don't you see how I blame myself? I should have said that the revolver was in the study all the time. That Mr Callis was here the day before he did it – and in the study too. Everyone knows he had no scruples. He must have been snooping about in the desk drawers, found the revolver, and put it in his pocket. The revolver provided him with the means – that's why he killed himself the day after he'd got hold of it.'

I knew immediately that the truth lay here. She would never lie to me or humour me. My exhaustion vanished in an access of almost impersonal curiosity. I wanted to put her into possession of more and more facts so that she could interpret to me the situation that I could not understand but which suddenly seemed to have been ordered in my favour, as though some patron deity had been working, unknown to me, on my behalf. Far off, in another world, was Laurence's bedroom and the drawer in his bedside chest.

'I thought Callis had been murdered,' I said, and the proposition seemed novel, obviously fallacious. 'I felt that I was responsible, Hindy.'

'Oh, Mr Harry,' she said warmly, 'you couldn't help him stealing your revolver. If it hadn't been that it would have been something else. You mustn't let yourself have any qualms, you really mustn't. You'll never get well.'

Might I recover? The image came to me of myself sitting up in bed, reading, the room still, the next day with its routine of shaving, eating, the office, rather boringly but not unpleasantly ahead. Could life turn and offer me its un-hideous profile again? I realized that I had been living for days, weeks, an existence for which human beings had been constructed to bear only minutes, hours.

Thelma Hind was saying nervously: 'That's why I came to look for you, Mr Harry.'

'I'm sorry,' I said. 'I wasn't listening.'

'Mr Laurence knew that you'd left the revolver behind,' she said. 'I can't understand why *he* didn't tell the detectives. Is it awful of me to say that?'

When I had moved to Luxor Street the desk had not been in the study, only the little early-Victorian bureau with the marble top that my father had always used. Laurence must have found the revolver after I had gone and put it in the desk drawer. It was strange that I had not packed the revolver with its associated underclothing. Perhaps even before I had left Laurence had come across the revolver and placed it in safe keeping.

'I can't understand it, either,' I said. She went to the banisters and looked over. 'What's the matter?' I asked her.

'Nothing,' she said. 'Nothing.'

The problem fascinated me. 'Do you really think Callis would open the drawers in someone else's desk? Supposing you or Laurie had walked in? Was he left alone in the study?'

'I don't remember,' said Miss Hind. 'I've been trying to remember. But he must have been.'

'Unless Laurie gave him the gun.' It was the ridiculous, random answer that somehow just filled the squares and took in the skeleton letters already there. What one had to do was to work it back to the clue to find out why it could be right.

'Yes,' she said. 'Unless Mr Laurence provided the means.'

Once again I began to be frightened. We had been talking too long in this dark corner, with its hiding places, its accessibility: Hindy had been too long away from her duties downstairs. I said to her: 'Hadn't you better go back?'

'It's all right,' she said with embarrassment. 'He thinks I've gone home.'

'He?' I said, but there was no need for her to answer. And then I had to ask her: 'Was Callis getting money out of him?'

'There were those advances,' she whispered.

'No, not those. Privately.'

'Why should he give Mr Callis money privately?' But the question was half-hearted and I saw her head involuntarily turn and look along the passage towards the stairs to the half landing which, however, curved away so that the door of my old room was out of our sight.

Still I did not understand. If only I could go away to a quiet place, take a sheet of paper and fountain pen and work it all out. . . . My mind could not rid itself of the picture of Laurence handing the revolver to Callis across the plate glass of the desk and saying to him, in words that were more real than I could have imagined: 'You mustn't be afraid.'

Thelma Hind said: 'What will you do, Mr Harry?'

The picture vanished, and I tried to promote, from its place among my confused thoughts, the knowledge that Callis had not been murdered, that the machinery of my punishment had ceased to revolve, had never revolved. What would I do?

'I don't know, Hindy.' What precisely was it that prevented me from walking downstairs, out of the house, to what had suddenly become the harbour of my flat?

She seemed to know how my mind worked. 'I must go home now,' she said. 'Perhaps you'd like to come with me as far as the tube.'

'Will you tell the police about the revolver, Hindy?'

'Of course. I shall ring up from home.'

'I think I ought to stay and speak to my brother, Hindy.'

Again she accepted it as though she knew that I had to say it. 'Yes, Mr Harry.' She hesitated, took a step forward, returned, and then said: 'Good night.'

'Good night, Hindy. Thank you.'

'Oh,' she said from the top of the stairs, 'don't thank me. I ought to ask you to forgive me. I was weak.' She hurried down, and as soon as she was out of my sight the fear seized me and I went after her, as though I were a child and she someone whom I could providentially get to accompany me through the dark.

Of course I must leave with her: what madness had made me say otherwise?

At the bend of the stairs I heard voices and stopped, paralysed. When I peered down into the hall I could see Laurence with his back to the front door and Miss Hind before him, buttoning her over-green, over-fur-trimmed coat, talking rather too volubly. The words were not distinguishable. Then Laurence smiled, and opened the door: Miss Hind went by him quite easily into the yellow and black of the square. Laurence shut and locked the door behind her and I wondered what I should see, when he turned, on his unguarded face.

But it was only the face I knew already. The body below it stood for a moment and then walked into the dining-room: the body had a thickness round the hips, a delicacy of movement, incongruous but significant and inevitable. The light went on and off and Laurence came out, shutting the door behind him. I saw him go along to the garden room, leaving the hall to the guardianship of the stone god whose worn face at the foot of the stairs I had so often avoided, descending alone in the twilight. In a few minutes Laurence would have looked in all the rooms on the ground floor and would start on the first: I remembered the methodical and meticulous little books of receipts and expenditure he had kept when he was in his teens. But still I didn't move. When I was a very little boy I sometimes knew that he was behind the statue, waiting to spring out suddenly with a loud cry, but I would still continue down the stairs. I had taken his teasing persecution of me as one of life's natural phenomena, and I had never thought that it arose from hatred of me. Often we were very close, absorbed in some mutual pursuit, despite the disparity in our ages. But after all, it was only hatred that he had felt, so that years later when the opportunity arose, when my balance had gone, he had played this enormous, unbelievable deception – handing the gun to Callis, like fire to a child, putting the abundant barbiturate in my way as though we both knew that I had an incurable cancer.

If this had been the only guilt round my neck I think I could have gone down to the hall, hammered on the door, roused the servants, demanded to be let out, risked the police, the white-coated attendants. As it was, it was with the strenuous but feeble steps of a nightmare that I turned and went up the stairs, past the drawing-room, the room where Adrian Rossiter perhaps lay asleep in his boredom, the room where my father had died and eventually to the room at the very top of the house.

6

The table-tennis table had replaced the model railway layout, just as the railway had replaced the womb-like system of chairs and rugs into which we had once wriggled cosily with our woolly toys. The table-tennis table was still there, under the green-shaded lights, the net slack and drooping, no doubt because Joe still made an occasional habit of sleeping on it. At the end I always used to take, the ceiling sloped to the uncurtained window that looked out east over the house-tops towards the faintly orange glow in the sky of the West End. I closed the door behind me and should have turned the lights off but was afraid to. I slid down the bolts of the glass double doors that opened on to the flat part of the roof, and tried the handle. The doors opened but I did not go out. I shut the doors but kept them unbolted.

Self-consciously, as though I were on a stage, I put a cigarette between lips that I felt were slightly trembling. The smoke coiled into the conical rays of the lights. Here was the way of escape, but perhaps I should not have to use it. The edge of the flat roof was guarded by a row of squat little pillars, surmounted by a narrow parapet. The next house in the square was three yards away, with a similar roof, a similar parapet. It was perfectly possible to jump from one parapet to the other: years ago I had – filled with nausea, envious, responsible, hoping he would fall, praying that he would get there and back in safety – watched Laurence do it when we had been illegally alone together on the roof.

It could be that I was mistaken in thinking that Laurence was suspiciously searching the house for me. Perhaps when he found that I was not in his room he would imagine that my malady had once more set me wandering, taken me out of the house while he was engaged with Miss Hind. But whatever I tried to tell myself

I knew that now, at this minute, I ought to be across the gap, on the fire escape, out of the square, far from this dangerous house. Still I smoked, my eyes on the shining green table, the chill of the room slowly working on my moist hands, my burning face. All at once I thought of Callis, that after all he wasn't a phoney, that underneath the ugly face, the careless clothes, the obnoxious manner, he had truly suffered: that in his mind there had been some catastrophic fault which even money could not heal.

I went to the doors and opened them again. Over the black key-like shapes of the house tops an orange-gold moon was rising in a dramatic and monolithic arrangement of clouds, as unreal as a picture post-card. The memory of the past came to me as an almost actual smell of cigar smoke, my father's entry at dusk into our childish world, and a sensation of grubbiness and dishevelment against his white cuffs and grooming. The pain of his terrible death was physical, a pain that could be borne only by a restless movement, a frantic projection of thought on to a wildly irrelevant subject.

I heard the turning of the handle of the other door and moved quickly and guiltily back to the great toy cupboard on the high wall opposite the window. In the play Kirillov presses his body between the cupboard and the wall: I had no time to do that. Laurence's eyes fell on me as soon as he opened the door, but I saw him start.

He said: 'Harry, what on earth are you doing up here?' There was nothing in his voice but wonder and solicitude. For a moment I was deceived into thinking that all he had said to me was true, that he was not acting: I felt myself slipping back into the pit of utter despair.

'I can't do it,' I said.

'I went to my bedroom. . . .' But he could not keep up the spell: I could distinguish beneath his manner, as though it were a bad disguise, his real emotions. He shut the door behind him and came to the edge of the table. The lights illuminated his hands: between the joints of each finger was a rectangle of sparse black hair and on the little finger of his left hand a silver ring set with a topaz. From his breast upwards he was in shadow, but stray beams caught the lenses of his eyes and his face shone palely.

'Why do you hate me?' Though I had not intended it nor thought I felt it even, the words came out charged with feeling, forced through some distorting bottleneck.

'Hate you, Harry?' The hands made a gesture.

'You want me to die.'

'It's the last thing I want.' The voice was more than ever vibrant. 'I've only tried to think of you. If I'd seen any other way out of this frightful disaster I would have helped you to take it. You're ill, Harry. I don't think you know what you're saying, or how much it pains me.'

'I never took the revolver to Luxor Street,' I said; the words were grape skins that had to be forced from my dry palate.

He took a step round the table. 'You're deluded,' he said harshly.

'It was here all the time. You showed Callis the way to suicide just as you showed it to me an hour ago.'

'This is preposterous.' Now he was close to me, and his hand gripped my forearm and shook it. 'Do you want me to telephone the police? Do you want them to come and arrest you, try you, hang you?'

The contact with him alarmed me. I pulled myself free. 'You won't telephone the police. Hindy saw the revolver in your desk.'

'I see,' he said. The shadow once more covered him. 'Your delusions are complete. I can't do anything more for you, Harry.'

I had to tell him everything. I said: 'I think Callis knew about your deserter friend.'

I heard him take in a breath but the word that came when he let it out was only, 'Ah.' There was a long silence. Then he said, as though he were not my brother: 'You're insane all right, but you'll never establish it. You're too intelligent, Harry, and they don't find the intelligent ones insane. You were jealous of Max Callis and you shot him. Madness, of course, but only the kind of madness that makes murderers, not that saves them. And all this nonsense about the revolver and blackmail. . . . You are quite evil.'

As soon as the word came out I remembered. The night-light balancing its grotesque shadows, Laurence's arms round me in bed, and his voice telling of his dreams or his visions – the man who was forcing the sin of murder on him, the man whose place had at last been taken by the apparition of a woman. When I used to repeat to myself the Lord's Prayer before getting into bed, the word 'evil', whose meaning I did not understand, was represented by the figures Laurie had made terrifyingly real for me; so that my prayer meant, 'Deliver me from the squat, bearded, approaching man, the veiled woman.'

Laurence said: 'I'm glad you came up to this room. I want to show you something.' He walked towards the glass doors. 'Come out here.'

I began to tremble. 'No,' I said.

'I'm going to blow away your delusions about me for ever,' he said. 'Come out on to the roof.'

As the man who has to submit to some excoriation of the throat and at first opens his mouth a little way, hoping that will be enough but knowing otherwise, I went to the open doorway. Laurence had walked half way to the parapet. The moon now had freed itself from the low clouds and was burning, incandescent, almost full, in the still sky. A shadow stretched from Laurence's feet and at last dissolved in the light from the door.

'Daren't you come to the parapet?' Laurence called, his voice seeming to fill all the air. He came back to me. 'I don't wonder. Do you remember that father used to stand with us on top of it when he was telling us the names of the buildings that could be seen from here?'

I remembered, and felt the crepitations of a deeper cold than the cold of the air. But I said with a bravado that amazed and terrified me: 'Why should you think I'm afraid of the parapet?' And walked past him until my shins pressed the little pillars and I could see the perspective of the walls converging towards the blur of darkness below. A small sickness that was not all vertigo settled below my solar plexus. When I felt that he was close behind me I turned and took a step away from the precipice.

'I think you know why,' he said. He paused until the interval was scarcely to be borne. 'When you were eight years old you confessed to me that while you stood there with father you wished he would fall – that you wanted to push him, that you would have done if you hadn't stepped down and run back into the nursery.'

'No,' I said. 'No.'

'Eight years old! My poor Harry, you were all but a murderer then. A parricide. Do you think I can possibly take any notice of your prevarications about Callis?'

I sank to the parapet and buried my face in my hands. I had time in my mind to wonder whether this was all acting, and then with the thought of my father and his death came a flood of realization that at first I imagined irrelevant to the hour and the place, to Laurence's feet which I could see through my fingers pacing out the little swift itinerary of an animal in a cage.

Laurence did not hate me: he merely wanted me to die. I saw, as though it were a film, the front of the office in New Square, the piles of snow, as grubby as a piece of icing from a boy's pocket, in the gutter, Laurence and I still in our strange funeral garb. In the dark room at the back of the ground floor, Theodore Simmons, father's solicitor, had taken instructions from Laurence while my eyes, already detached from my emotions, wandered round the bookshelves, the lifeboat calendar, the Spy prints, the empty tea cup, back again and again to the stiff sheets bound with green silk of my father's will on which I had seen, when Simmons went through it with us, my father's familiar signature looking as vivid as if he had been still alive instead of unbelievably dead. There had not been much to go through. The repayment of my father's share in his firm was, of course, dealt with by the partnership deed. After some legacies to Baker, other servants and office employees, and to charities, and the devise of the house to Laurence, the will had left the residue of the estate to Laurence and me equally. The knowledge that I was rich had come to me merely as an added burden. 'A commendably brief will,' Theodore Simmons had said. 'Of course, you are a small family, but commendably brief, nevertheless.' Yes, we were a small family, and since I had never had either the impulse or the reason to make a will myself, on my death my property would pass to Laurence.

The feet stopped a yard from me, pointing towards me. 'It's no use hiding your face,' he said in a driving voice.

But I went on hiding it, overwhelmed by the ambiguity of my thoughts. For if Laurence could scheme my death to inherit my riches, how much more plain was it that I had killed my father to get them. Every motive I could attribute to Laurence must, since we were brothers, be my own. Callis's end now appeared to me as absurd a concern as a monstrous childish worry to the child grown up.

Laurence said: 'It's no use, Harry. You must face it that you are the man you are – with this flaw born in you.'

I wondered why he stopped here when the logic which would take him to accusing me of father's murder was so elementary. I saw that my father's illness had shouted a suspicion that Laurence – not a fool like Dr Riddell – could not fail to hear now even if at the time its outrageousness, like the hiding place of the purloined letter, had blunted his faculties to it. I looked up at him, haloed by the light from the nursery, the chimney pots like a row of Caligaris over his head. I talked quickly to prevent his mind from following in the track that mine had cut. 'I'll give myself up,' I lied. 'I've come to the end of my courage, Laurie. I can't take your way out. I'll go to the police station at the bottom of Kensington Church Street. It's terrible to burden you with my presence here – you've been marvellous, Laurie. . . .'

I could see that he didn't believe me. He came very close to me and looked down into my eyes. He said: 'But you have no control of yourself at all. You can't be sure that when you walk out of this house you won't go into hiding again, that you won't still be a danger.'

He was so close that I felt myself forced to hold on to the parapet: the pressure of the flaking stucco brought back the atmosphere of my father's presence. The doors from the nursery to the roof were always, because of the danger, kept locked except when my father came up to us. To be here on the parapet was to be with my father, to be possessed of the impulse to thrust him over the edge.

Time and again my father had come out with us and remained unharmed. That murderous wish, if it had ever seriously been mine, had been only in the mind. I had never touched him. My heart beat faster with excitement. And, as the sun comes out finally from a cloud and the faintly suggested or imagined shadows of tree or house all at once are clarified, filled with uncompromising black, these baffling and painful events, my whole life, lay plain to my understanding.

I rose and saw Laurie not through the eyes of a brother, but as one gazes uncomprehendingly, fascinatedly, at some notorious figure brought by authority into public cynosure – a figure whose face, hands, clothes even, seem steeped in some element from another order of material existence.

'I never touched him,' I said.

'You shot him,' said Laurence. 'You had no need to touch him.'

'Not Callis,' I said. 'Father. I didn't harm him here on the roof. And I didn't poison him. It follows, you see.'

'What are you talking about?' Laurence said, in a terrible voice. 'Poison? Poison?'

Since I was guiltless, only my brother, whose blood and motives were mine, could take my place. As in a symphony of Sibelius, at first there are only wisps and hints of melody, but at last comes plain, making the whole work clear, the extensive, intelligible theme. 'It was arsenic,' I said tremblingly, 'wasn't it?'

He took a stride towards the door. 'It will have to be the police,' he said. 'This is raving.'

'How could you bring yourself to make him suffer?' Tears made my words gross. 'And only for money. He would have given you your bloody share if you'd wanted it so much.'

He said: 'What makes you think that?' And he came back to me slowly, his head inclined as though he were involved in some abstruse calculation. After he had worked it out he said: 'Yes, I hate you, Harry – if that isn't too strong a word. I detest you, anyway, your virtue, your normality. The average man, the ideal son. The only sympathy I've ever felt for you has been during these last months: a fellow feeling. Perhaps in your neurosis you've come to understand a little the realities of living for someone who isn't a cipher, who isn't crusted with the conventions that man has invented to keep life bearable. Perhaps you've begun to understand people like Callis – and me.'

My brain was so packed with these awful connexions and revelations that if I took one thought in, it had to replace another, like an object in a full suitcase. 'No, I don't understand you, Laurie. Mine's been an aberration of the mind – yours is an aberration of action. To put the gun into Callis's hand and to tell him – you must have told him – the formula that would make it natural for him to hold it to his head. And to make father vomit, vomit—' I made blindly for the light of the nursery.

I felt his arm, hard as iron, round my shoulder. He swung me back in my path so that I stumbled against him, smelling under the faint perfume the odour of his sweat, as alien as an animal's.

'Where are you going?' he said. His breathing was loud in my ears, as though we were in an erotic embrace.

'I don't know.' I was very frightened.

'Nothing can be proved.'

'No,' I said.

'Even against you.' He dropped his arm but I did not dare to move away. 'Because you aren't really sure, are you, Harry, that you didn't kill Callis and father?'

'One thing I'm sure of,' I said, loathing him, wanting him to suffer, 'I'm not harbouring a little pansy deserter in my flat.'

Almost, it seemed, before he had time to hear the words his fist came up across my mouth and nose, and as I felt the dull heaviness of the blow change slowly to pain and the blood fill my nostrils I had a strange sense of the inevitable repetitive patterns of life, for this had happened before in our childhood, my blood flowing on the pillows of our common bed, and Laurence watching it, his anxiety long minutes behind his anger and triumph. I backed away from him, knowing that never again would he feel anxiety for me.

'You smug bastard,' he said, and the words on his lips were as sordid as the idea of the participation of his elegant body and brain in those private pleasures which must rule so large a part of his being. Yes, he had hated me from the day he had obscurely known that my mother carried a rival to his power, through my birth and her death, and the long divergence of our two ways. And I saw, as though I were an outsider, his monstrous existence – his extravagance, his fear of blackmailers, his hours of darkness with the vulgar and rapacious, his reputation in the world of art, his imaginative magazine, his delicate and aspiring prose, his coarsening and handsome body, his desire for money and power.

He stood bathed in the pale-blue light like some creature of the theatre.

'All the same,' I said, through my numb and thickening lips, 'arsenic is indestructible. An exhumation would show it. And however careful the murderer has been they always seem able to link him with his poison.' As I spoke I realized that now I had no need to accept his assumption of physical power over me. The days of our childhood, before convention had grown over the desire to express our antagonisms in blows and scratchings, had ended before I had been able to match his strength and will. I half hoped that he would come up to me again, menacingly, so that I could show him the profound change in our state. But he stood immobile, as though I had not been there, absorbed, withdrawn.

Once more I started for the open doors, like a boy who imagines that his otherwise occupied master has forgotten the punishment he promised him. Somewhere there was a life which was not all pain and it seemed almost within my reach. But in his trance Laurence moved surely over to cut me off.

He said: 'I know why you came up here. To escape. Across the Gap.'

I had forgotten the name we used to give to it. I said nothing.

'Well, why don't you go?'

The grotesque now seemed utterly natural. Since I had so easily imagined my own guilt it was with scarcely any effort of adjustment that I filled his mind with the thoughts that had burned in mine and moved his body in the violent uninhibited gestures that was their logical end. I had to get down from this stage, plunge myself into the commonplace life of the spectator that begins only as he rises from his seat when the ranting and blood has been hidden by the curtain.

'Why don't you?' he said again. 'Go on.' And he gave my shoulder a little push. It was like the first tiny diplomatic acerbity in the relations of two countries destined to exterminate each other.

'I'm going this way, Laurence,' I said, the bitterness rising physically in my mouth. And I took a step towards the doors.

Once again came the nudge against my body. It caught me off balance and was followed by another. To my astonishment and fear I found myself giving ground. 'No.' I said. 'No.' And while I gathered myself for the effort to circumvent him, for the action half-swerve, half-battering ram, that my body instinctively prepared itself for as if it had never forgotten its aptitude for football, I felt his whole height and weight alarmingly against me, like an underestimated force of nature. I was borne back until the parapet came up behind my knee, and it was only then that I realized that his hand was hard against the softness under my jaw and that the loud choking noises I could hear were my own.

He was grunting, and kept on saying as though it were a formula of excuse for this terrible scene: 'Get across the Gap then. Get across. Get across.'

Even then the diffidence and excessive concern for others I had shown all my life still operated. It was to save Laurence embarrassment and pain that I sank frantically to my knees, pulling him down with me, so that only my back was pressed against the narrow stonework, only my head felt the empty air of the dizzy space between the houses. Behind the dark hair ruffled round his great head I could see the yellow points of stars in the soft, powdered sky.

With one hand he was pushing against my jaw: the other was helping my trunk to rise higher on the parapet. Now I tried to cry out, but no sound came. I had never imagined that events like these would have to be played to their unimaginable conclusion: in spite of its continual experiences to the contrary the civilized mind always believes in the essential tameness and uneventfulness of existence. Quite suddenly, with an effort of will rather than physique, I slid from under him: his hand was wrenched from my throat, and his shoulder fell heavily against the stone. The heels and sides of my shoes scrabbled again and again over the flat lead of the roof as I tried to twist myself wholly round. He half rose to his feet, his arm came savagely round my neck, and for a sickening instant I plunged on top of him towards the darkness beyond the edge of the parapet. His knee drove up into my stomach and with a slow but frightful momentum I felt our bodies curve over a point of balance that was as narrow as a parapet. I clutched at the stone: its passage burned my finger tips.

And then he cried out. And again. His arm left my neck and

waved wildly in the air. His body arched in a strychnine-like
convulsion and all at once my hands were trying to get a grip
of the cloth of his suit as it tore through them. In a moment I
was changed from fear of him to fear for him. A button flicked
my fingers: and for what could have been only a split second I
felt his hip bone under my hand as I pressed him to the parapet.
Then, as unbelievable as the last irretrievable breath of the dying,
the catastrophe unfolded itself beneath my eyes. Beyond human
reach, Laurence fell into the darkness: not clearly, dream-like,
as years ago I had imagined it, but somehow hitting the wall of
the house, sprawling, dim. And now I saw that the edge of the
conservatory projected a corner to the place immediately below
where I leaned. It was this projection that the dark untidy bundle
struck, with a thud that brought the nausea to my cold lips, that
it stayed against, and even moved slowly against with one un-
annihilated part of itself.

7

I took my sickness and trembling across the leagues of empty
roof, trying to hasten. I became conscious of an excruciating
pain in my right hand and when I looked at it in the light of the
nursery saw the nails of my two middle fingers torn in half, blood
oozing from the quick. But I saw them only half comprehend-
ingly, thinking over and over again of those destined physical
motions on the parapet.

At the door of the nursery appeared a figure I knew but could
not place, as though he were a character from my past. 'Oh,
it's you,' said this figure in a frightened, squeaking voice. 'I say,
what's happening? What was that shouting?'

I stared at him and remembered the remote fantastic time
when I believed I had murdered my father and Max Callis. I said:
'My brother has fallen from the roof. Go and ring up for the
ambulance. Quickly. And the police.'

Adrian Rossiter's fingers went to his bad teeth. 'Christ!' he
said. And then: 'You've a nerve. I'm ringing up for no bloody
police. What d'you take me for?'

I brushed past him and started down the stairs. He followed me like a cowed domestic animal. 'Is he dead?' he asked. I felt him pluck at my jacket. 'Are *you* going to get the coppers here?' he said. 'What's going to happen to little me?'

'Oh flick off,' I said.

'You're a very rude man,' he said. 'I certainly won't bother to stay here now.' And I continued my way down alone.

In the hall the statue presented its eroded grief-stricken image: by it, the maid who had opened the door to me showed a counterpart mask, uncertain, alarmed. She met me with eyes begging for reassurance, a way through the cataclysm.

I said to her: 'Call the ambulance.'

'Yes, sir,' she said. 'We heard it downstairs – '

But without waiting to listen I ran through the open door of the dining-room and, across its lighted space, saw the conservatory's shut glass doors like an unopened letter of terrible news.

As the sad and exhausted relative calls the undertakers to remove his long responsibility, I felt that soon there might return to me the forgotten conditions for happiness. Under the disfiguring scab of these days the healing work had improbably, slowly, miraculously proceeded. I stopped and grasped the carver's chair that, like a throne, first my father and then Laurence had occupied. I saw clearly that this final event, too, was as ambiguous as all the others; that now I was guilty of my brother's death as well. But I could at last put a limit on my guilt, the normal limit that makes life possible at all in the cruel world. To the morality of the authorities my actions on the roof were justifiable to save myself. The investigation would uncover the trail left by Laurence's guilt – his purchase of poison, his opportunities of administering it on that Christmas Day, his inherited wealth. They would see his hand in Callis's suicide – the gentle blackmail, the opportune gift of my revolver, the subsequent lies. All the themes, which time and my mind had so confusingly combined and developed, would be disentangled and played over in their right order and in simple form.

I thought that when the police and the orderlies arrived I might even be able to go with them the last few yards to the horror in the green and black gloom beyond the doors.